Give a Little Love
A Jordan Family Story

Rhonda McKnight

Also by Rhonda McKnight

Live A Little: A Jordan Family Story
Breaking All The Rules: Second Chances - Book 1
Unbreak My Heart: Second Chances – Book 2
Secrets and Lies
An Inconvenient Friend
What Kind of Fool
A Woman's Revenge

Table of Contents

Acknowledgements

My readers - You encouraged me to get back in front of the laptop for something other than play. Thanks for loving my work and encouraging me to give you another story. A special shout-out to my Facebook Group. You Black Girls Rock! I appreciate your feedback and encouragement. Thanks also for giving me all the hip lingo. You ladies keep me in the know.

Thanks to my author buddies Sherri Lewis, Tia McCollors and Tiffany L. Warren for reminding me that writing is my passion and a my gift. I'd forgotten that. I also appreciate the encouragement and advice from other authors in my circle: Michelle Lindo-Rice, Makasha Dorsey, Keleigh Crigler-Hadley, Cherlisa Starks-Richardson, Vanessa Miller and Michelle Stimpson.

I have the best editor in the world, Felicia Murrell of The Bee Company (http://www.yzcounsel.com) Felicia thank you for the amazingly fast job you did to help me get this out in time. I appreciate you so much.

Hi Ma! Can't write a book without acknowledging my mother, Bessie McKnight or my sons, Aaron and Micah. Love you!

Rhonda McKnight

Chapter 1

"Jesus is the reason for the season." The radio D.J. from Love 101 FM's smooth voice crooned from the stereo speakers on the table next to her. Brooke Jordan flipped the power button to off before he could say another word. Even though Jesus was the reason for the season, her Christmas was going to be *stank* with a capital S. There was no getting around that fact.

Brooke pushed the plantation shutters on the windows open to let in the sounds of the reggae influenced Christmas music rising up from below. She couldn't believe she was spending Christmas week in Montego Bay, Jamaica. It would have been perfect if she wanted to be here, but she didn't. She wasn't on vacation. This wasn't a pleasure trip. Brooke had drawn the short straw in a staff meeting, so she was stuck working. *Stank*, she thought, *stank on steroids.*

She leaned against the sill of the window, closed her eyes and inhaled a long, intoxicating breath of ocean air. Every aspect of the island was paradise: the weather, the ocean views and the food. There was no doubt about it. But no place was really paradise when you wanted to be somewhere else. Brooke opened her eyes and squinted to see a couple further down the beach. They lay in the sand, making out or maybe even making love. Honeymooners, she knew. She'd seen them arrive a few days ago. Brooke watched as they arrived and others left. She remembered how it was for her when she had honeymooned on an island. She'd been in love like that. She had made love on the beach and then less than two years later, she was signing divorce papers. She tried not to hold it against the entire Caribbean, but there were too many reminders of her loss. She wanted to go home. Today!

Brooke's cell phone vibrated in her pocket and then she heard a chirp. She recognized the familiar beeping ringtone she'd assigned to her parents. She answered. "Hello. You're early." Brooke noted it was seven a.m., which meant it was six o'clock in Charlotte.

"I wanted to get you before you left for work."

Resting an arm on the windowsill she said, "You made me nervous for a moment. I thought there might have been some kind of emergency."

"There is an emergency," Evelyn Jordan replied. "My daughter isn't going to be home for Christmas Eve dinner."

Brooke sighed. No one was more disappointed than she that on the only holiday her family emphatically made sure not to miss being together, she was four hours by plane away. There was just no way to get to Charlotte, actually have dinner with the family, and get back to the island on the same day. She had to work on Christmas Day.

"I'll be home for New Year's Eve," Brooke offered, knowing it was no consolation prize for the annual dinner with her grandmother, parents, six siblings, in-laws and nieces and nephews. She would be the only one missing this year. Her brother, Gage, had returned from a tour in Afghanistan and would be with the family for the first time in two years. Her heart ached and she knew it wasn't just about the family dinner. She'd been away from her family and friends for far too long. With the ridiculous hours she had to put in on the project, she hadn't had much time to even socialize and meet other people. Not that she probably would have taken the time to do that either. Brooke was on the verge of sliding into a state of depression and she knew it.

"Is the company sponsoring a dinner for the staff?"

Brooke moved through the large living room of the corporate apartment and entered the kitchen to start the coffeemaker.

"No. Everyone is gone. I mean the people who are still here live on the island. The ex-pats are home. There are two analysts and me. We don't need more. We babysit the system."

"Well, maybe you can make dinner. You could invite the analysts. Is one of them nice looking?"

Brooke shook her head. Not more match making. "Mother." Using mother was a sign that she was getting annoyed.

"I'm sorry. I was wondering if a change in environment might…" her mother stopped herself. "Never mind that. You could invite them anyway. People get lonely during the holidays."

Brooke didn't respond. People get lonely at Christmas. Forget people. She was lonely. Last year, she was married. Now, she was divorced. Last year, she was with her family. This year, she would be alone. Last year, she was pregnant. This year, she had no child. She didn't care about what other people needed. She had needs of her own.

"Sweetheart, don't they kind of work for you?" her mother's voice broke through her thoughts.

"Not technically. I'm the team leader. It's not the same as being the boss." Brooke fought to keep a sigh inside. She had explained the nature of her work to her mother several times, but for some reason the details weren't processing. "Anyway, we can't eat together. First off, one has a girlfriend he's spending time with and the other guy is, I don't know, anti-social. I hardly know him. Secondly, if I'm home, they're managing the system. We have to be there for the eighteen hours of the day that we're up."

"It seems such a waste not to be able to entertain. You have that big place and the kitchen is lovely."

Brooke did a visual sweep of the space. Her mother was right. She was in a two-bedroom apartment that actually slept six adults comfortably. The kitchen was fully equipped with every modern convenience a person could use. The community had three swimming pools, a hot tub, sauna, a fitness center and it had the added bonus of being directly on the beach with gulf views from nearly every window she'd seen. The company had spared no expense and Brooke was glad. The hotel she had lived in for the first few weeks had gotten old fast.

"I'm not interested in cooking for myself. Freeze a plate for me. I'll eat it when I get home. There are more than enough restaurants for me to stop in at. You know I love the local food."

Her mother conceded. "Okay, sweetie, I know you have to get to the office, so I'll let you go. What time will you be home this evening?"

"Same as always. Around eight."

"You've been working too hard."

"I make good money and I like my job. I can Skype with you guys during dinner. It'll be like I'm there."

Brooke heard the smile in her mother's voice. "It will. I'll take that. Your grandmother reminded me that I need not complain. I have living children. That's a blessing."

She smiled at her grandmother's wisdom and the not so subtle message behind it. "Stop complaining when you're blessed." That's what she always said when Brooke moaned about something.

The coffee maker beeped and she received a text message from her driver that he was outside. "Gotta go. Love you, Mama and tell Daddy I love him too."

"Oh, Brooke, there's one more thing."

She knew it. Her mother never called this early in the morning unless something was up. "Sam called."

Brooke rolled her eyes.

"I didn't want to bring it up. It's not the first time." Her mother paused. "I thought you should know."

Brooke swallowed her contempt and tried to keep her voice even. "Thanks, Mama. I received an email. I'll go ahead and see what it says."

"That's probably a good idea," her mother said. "Have a good day, baby."

Brooke forced a smile into her voice. "I will."

They ended the call. She'd lied to her mother. Brooke had already deleted the email without opening it, and she'd deleted the others that came before that one. She pushed thoughts of Sam Riley from her mind the same way she pushed the delete button. She was not going to let rancid memories ruin her day.

She poured her coffee, popped the lid on her travel mug, grabbed her bags and left the apartment.

"Good mornin', Ms. Brooke." Desmond, the company's fulltime driver, opened the door to the company van and helped her into the back row.

"You're cheery this morning," Brooke replied getting settled into her seat.

He closed the door and went around to the front and climbed inside. "It's almost Christmas," Desmond shrieked happily. "Can you believe it'll be here in less than two days?"

Brooke took a long sip of her coffee and bit her lip after she felt the sting of the burn. It was still too hot. "I've never been away from home for Christmas, so it doesn't really feel like it to me."

Desmond shrugged like her woes meant nothing. "Christmas is wherever you are. You get a tree and play some Christmas music and make a little holiday for yourself."

Brooke chuckled. "A tree?"

"They have plenty in the market. If you want, I can pick one out and set it up for you when you come home this evening. It's no trouble."

Brooke smiled. Desmond very respectful and professional, but he had been trying to get in her apartment for some reason or another ever since she arrived on the island.

"There's a nice tree in the lobby and another out on the beach. We have one at work that I can enjoy too. It's not a big deal." She pressed her coffee cup against her lips and her lie and looked out the window for the remainder of the drive from her apartment to the office building. The trip was less than three miles, but it took thirty minutes because Montego Bay's traffic was gridlocked. Just like it was at home in Charlotte. Where there was work, there was congestion. She surmised you couldn't escape it.

They turned off of Sunset Boulevard onto Southern Cross Boulevard. Desmond pulled in front of the tall, 55,000 square foot complex that was the home for Global Computer Systems. GCS provides business process outsourcing and information technology solutions for commercial and government clients. Brooke's position as business analyst was to maintain the servers that processed electronic benefit card transactions for a government nutrition program. The client's customers had access to the benefits on their cards 24 hours a day, so the system had to be online 24-7 or it was a customer service nightmare.

They'd had those nightmares in the past. In order to ensure that the company didn't lose the government contract, GCS went through a massive technological upgrade in all the offices where they outsourced, which included this location.

Desmond opened the door on her side. Brooke stepped out and reached in for her bags.

"Would you like me to come get you for lunch?"

"No thanks, I'll get something up the street," she replied referring to the multitude of area restaurants she had to choose from.

"You text me if you change your mind about that tree."

She smiled. "Not likely, even if I were inclined, I don't have time."

"You do keep long hours, but at least you have some more help today."

Brooke wasn't sure what he meant by that. She tilted her head forward. "More help?"

"I picked a gentleman up at the airport last night."

Brooke wasn't aware of anyone else joining them. She wondered who had been given the daunting task of showing up the day before Christmas Eve. She knew she was being replaced in a few days so she could go home for a week, possibly for good. But she'd assumed the coworker that was replacing her wouldn't arrive until after Christmas. She also knew it was a woman, not a man.

She was way too curious to wait to find out who the mystery person was. She took a few steps toward

Desmond and asked, "Do you remember his name?"

"I don't. I was told to meet him and hold up the company card," Desmond said. "It was late and he had to take a connection in from Kingston, so he was tired. He fell asleep in the car on the way from the airport."

Brooke nodded. If he'd flown to Kingston, he hadn't come from the Charlotte office.

Desmond continued. "He was here before, I think. But, he either walked to work or rented a car. I didn't drive him."

Brooke shrugged. "I guess I'll find out today."

"In a few minutes," Desmond added. "He asked for an even earlier call than you, so he's already here."

Brooke nodded again. "Thanks for the heads up. I'll see you later."

Desmond smiled. As was his habit, he climbed in and waited for her to clear the entrance of the building. As she was coming in, Brooke caught sight of a woman that she'd seen many times in the square near the restaurants and shopping areas. She appeared to be homeless on most days, choosing to sit on the ground or lie on the waist high concrete walls that enclosed the main walking areas. Two of the security guards had her, one under each arm and were escorting her out of the building.

One of them tipped his hat and the other greeted her, "Good morning, Ms. Jordan. I already turned the key in the elevator, so you can go right up."

"What's going on?" Brooke felt sorry for the

woman. She looked like they were manhandling her a bit.

"She knows there's no trespassing," the other guard replied.

"Wait." Brooke stopped in front of them. She reached into her handbag and took out some Jamaican dollars she'd had converted from U.S. currency. It was more than enough to feed the woman for several days.

"Ma'am, no need," the guard stated.

"I know you're doing your job, but please turn her loose," Brooke insisted. They did as they were instructed. Brooke took the woman's hand and pressed the money into it. "Get something to eat okay."

The woman looked down at the bills and cackled. "I thank you, Ms. Brooke, but I'm not hungry."

Brooke was taken back. Her first name. "How do you know---?"

"I heard the people you work with call you that," she said. "You've got a good heart. God is going to bless you with love."

Brooke opened her mouth to speak, but then closed it when she realized she didn't really have anything to say. Brooke was a bit uncomfortable with the lady's words, especially since she was a stranger that appeared to need someone to speak into her own disheveled life, but she wasn't going to assume that God wasn't using her. What was that scripture her grandmother quoted about "entertaining angels unaware"? So even though she'd simply wanted to make sure the woman ate and wasn't thrown out like trash by the security guards, Brooke paused to consider the stranger's words.

"Any idea where I'm going to find this love?" Brooke asked as she fought to hide the hint of sarcasm that threatened to coat her tone.

"You've already found it," the woman replied, "just give a little and life will give back."

Brooke had no idea what she could be talking about. Other than giving out of her wallet as she just had, there wasn't any other opportunity for her to share with anyone. Brooke nodded her understanding and watched the woman push through the revolving door and exit onto the street.

One of the guards escorted her to the waiting elevator and continued to hold the doors open while she stepped in.

"She's a crazy lady. Been cuckoo since I was a kid. Keep your money the next time."

Brooke supposed the guards were right. They would certainly know better than she. But her grandmother had taught her that if we have the time of day for a dog, we have it for each other. Besides, the money was nothing. She made plenty.

The elevator doors closed. She pushed the button for the fourth floor of the building where the offices for I.T. were housed. The main server was on the basement level. The three intervening floors comprised a call center. Those spaces were empty today, because it was Sunday. Very few call center staff worked on Sunday and those that did were in the

United States offices.

Brooke heard her cell phone beep. She reached into her purse to remove it and felt a sharp bump against the bottom of the elevator car right before it paused. The elevator seemed to reboot and start again. She made a mental note to tell security to contact building maintenance and a second note to remind herself to use the other elevator until they fixed the problem. She looked down at her phone, opened the text message and read the words:

Aren't you usually at your desk by now?

Her heart started racing. She cleared the screen and dropped the phone back into her purse. The elevator doors opened. The late night arrival Desmond had spoken of…

"Good morning, Brooke. I've missed you."

Brooke let out a long breath. Christmas just got upgraded to ratchet.

Chapter 2

Marcus Thompson considered himself to be a good judge of people, but just like that, Brooke Jordan had him questioning himself. He'd missed her, but she had not missed him or at least it didn't appear she had. Either she should have been an actress or he had completely misread her. He preferred to believe the former. He hadn't flown seven hours to find out the latter.

"What are you doing here?" Brooke asked, not returning his hello and not waiting for an answer. She flew past him, making hasty steps to her office and paralyzing him for a moment in a haze of perfume that smelled sweet enough to wake a dead man.

Marcus followed, not only because the view from behind was mistletoe worthy, but also because he'd chosen the empty office right across from hers. He had to put a little run in his step to keep up with her. He couldn't imagine how a woman that was so petite compared to his six foot two inch height managed to move that much junk in the trunk on four-inch heels so quickly.

She entered the office, tossed her things on the desk and pushed the power button on her laptop.

Marcus cleared his throat. "I'm working."

Brooke raised her head and sliced him with annoyed eyes. "What?"

"You wanted to know what I'm doing here."

"I know you're working." She crossed her arms over her chest and rolled her eyes. "But why are you back? I thought you were gone."

"For good?"

"Something like that." She dropped her arms and bit her lip. "I meant…I didn't know you'd be back."

He cocked his head and smiled. "You didn't know I'd be back before the New Year, as in while you were still here?"

Brooke pursed her lips like she was not in the mood for the flirting. He smiled again. She had no idea how much it turned him on when she put up a fight, but they'd talk about that later, when he'd won the war.

"Operations decided you guys needed more support," he replied.

She dropped onto her chair and smiled slyly. "By operations, don't you mean you?"

Marcus flexed his shoulders a bit. It was true that he'd been promoted to Director of I.T. Operations since the last time he'd seen her. It was a nice little bump further up the management chain for him, but fortunately it was sideways, so it didn't put her in line as one of his direct reports. He did, however, have influence over how staff was allocated in her department and he planned to use that leverage if he had to.

Brooke crossed her arms over her chest again and her legs at the knees. Her skirt rode higher on her thighs revealing more of her delicious mocha brown skin. Completely unaware of the effect that one simple motion had on him, she continued. "I feel like I'm being spied on. If I'd known you were going to fly down here and micromanage my area I would have insisted I get to go home."

Marcus noticed the shadow of disappointment in her eyes. She had no idea that he was here on his own time and his own dime. No one in the management team thought it necessary for him to check on Brooke Jordan. Her reputation was strong. She could manage things down here with her eyes closed. He was on vacation for the holidays. This trip was about unfinished business between them. Business that distracted him to no end. Business that kept him up at night. Business that started on the evening when he'd fallen in love with Brooke Jordan.

She uncrossed her knees and slid her legs under her desk. "Since I am stuck here, I'd like to get my work done."

He lifted a brow. "Let me know when you go down to the server room. I'd like to go with you."

Annoyance flashed across her face. "Harold and I have it under control," she said referring to her coworker, Harold Green, one of the other analysts.

"I know you two are doing the split shift thing, so I let Harold go home already. He looked tired."

Brooke tapped the mouse and cleared the screensaver that filled her dormant computer screen and signed into the system. "I usually do my check at noon." She didn't give him the satisfaction of raising her eyes from the computer. That was okay, she'd be gazing in his eyes soon enough.

"I'll be right across the hall." He knew it was time to leave, but he hesitated. He had traveled too far and too long to see her again, to be in her presence to have to leave her already. Her sweet oval face and those deep-set almond shaped eyes had filled his thoughts, not to mention the bend of her long slender neck and that sexy mole over her eye. She had no idea that he'd framed a company Christmas party picture that included her and placed it on his desk, so he could look at her throughout the day. She had no idea how completely sprung, whupped, gone or whatever the young folks called it these days, he actually was. It was that one date. One night when she'd let down her hair and showed him who Brooke Jordan really was that he'd been unable to forget and he'd been holding on to as he bid his time before he could get back here and see her again.

"Did you need something?" she asked, interrupting his thoughts of her.

"No, I think that's all, Brooke." He turned to leave.

"Ms. Jordan."

He heard her voice behind him, but he could hardly believe the words that had come out of her mouth. He turned and raised a finger to pull his earlobe forward. "Excuse me?"

"I said, Ms. Jordan. I prefer you called me by my

professional title."

Marcus chuckled. "Professional title? I figured we were on a first name basis."

She crossed her arms over her chest yet again and rolled her neck a bit. "What made you think that?"

He furrowed his brow in response to her spiciness. "I don't know, maybe something like you putting your tongue in my mouth the last time I saw you." Her jaw dropped. Just the reaction he'd been looking for. He left her office. He knew she was probably steaming, boiling really. But he'd also knew he'd left her with something to think about...that kiss.

Chapter 3

Brooke thought she'd never get her lips to close again. The shock permanently locked her jaw durn near in her lap. How dare he imply that she had kissed him? He had initiated everything from the entire evening out to the kiss. Manipulated was probably a better word, because it fit with what he was doing right now. There was no reason for him to even be here. What did he think? He was going to fly down to Jamaica and get some holiday lovin'. He was sadly mistaken if he thought she was giving it up.

She stood, walked to the open door of her office, and closed it shut. She wrapped her arms around her waist and rested her back against the door. Marcus Thompson. God, she was hoping she would never see him again. Or, at the very least that she wouldn't see him for a very, very long time; like in the year 2050.

That kiss he'd mentioned had been the bane of her existence for the last couple of months. Because try as she might, she could not stop thinking about it. She'd hoped not seeing him every day would help, that his returning to the states would make it all okay. But the way she felt about him was akin to the lyrics of a sad love song, "No matter how far, no matter where you are, I'll still be thinking of you," or something pathetic like that.

She sighed, pushed her body off the door and returned to her chair. She had a big report to put together and now that she knew Marcus was on site she was not trying to come into the office tomorrow.

"Clear your head, girl. He's just a man and you've been down this road before," she said as she clicked on icons to open the files needed to merge the data for her report. She worked for a few minutes before she realized she was pulling information from the wrong spreadsheet. "Ugh!" she groaned. Brooke couldn't shake his image from her mind. He had a nice face. Good and handsome, strong looking with a square jaw and chin, sharp cheekbones and deep-set dark brown eyes. He kept his jet black hair cut short and neat, but even with the little on his head she could see it was oddly straight. The strands were thick which revealed there were more than curly-headed folks up in the family tree. It wasn't just his looks that were appealing. Marcus had something else…a kind of charismatic way about him that drew women, lots of them and way too many for her liking.

She surmised the real attractant was his smile. It was magnetic, durn near electrifying, but even those pearly whites were no match for his body. She'd seen him at the beach at a company sponsored barbeque party. Determined not to get her hair wet, she'd sat on the sand and watched him rise from the ocean like some kind of Water God with his ridiculously sculpted abs, hulking biceps and shoulders that had to have backed a line in some football game back in the day. Those muscles were all she could think about when she was with him. She growled like a pissed off puppy and tried to get back to work.

Thirty minutes had gone by and she realized she'd still done nothing. Since she wasn't working anyway, Brooke picked up her cell phone and dialed.

"This is Cree," her sister said upon answering. The phone Brooke used for long distance calls showed up as unknown listing, so she didn't get the recognition she was used to when her sister answered the phone.

"Hey Creesie. It's me." Brooke called her sister by her childhood nickname.

"Brooke? What's wrong?"

Brooke pulled the phone back from her ear. "Wrong, what makes you think something's wrong?"

"Uh, you're calling and you're at work. You never call from work."

"Yes, I do. I call when I'm at home."

"Yeah, in Charlotte, on your lunch break, but never since you landed in paradise."

"I've been too busy to call and it's expensive. Today, I've got a little lull and I thought of you."

"Okay, I repeat. What's wrong?"

Brooke smirked. "Stop trippin'."

"You don't do small talk, big sis, so I know you have something on your mind. What is it?"

"I'm going to miss you guys tomorrow."

"Aw-wah," Cree replied. Brooke could almost see that smushy face Cree made when she responded that way. "We're going to miss you too."

"It's lonely here. I don't have a tree and there aren't any presents and then I have the most annoying coworker."

"That Harold guy?"

"No, it's Marcus. He's back. He came in last night."

Cree laughed. "Get out of here. You're spending Christmas with that fine piece of dark chocolate."

"No, I said he was back for work."

"I thought you said he was gone and promoted."

"He was, but he's here."

"For what? Two days before Christmas."

"I don't know. I think he's trying to check up on me."

"Or check you out."

"Don't be ridiculous. We're coworkers."

"And yeah, that's how I met my man."

"The one for this week?" Brooke barbed. Her sister was a serial dater. She had a new man in tow about every fourteen days and no one held her attention long enough to get out of her sixty day breakup window.

"Ha, ha, ha. At least I date. You could use one yourself. How else will you get another husband?"

"Who says I want another husband?"

"Chile please, you don't let one monkey stop the show."

Her sister had a point. Brooke knew that. She didn't want to be an old maid. She wanted kids, but at thirty-six she was quickly moving towards the category of spinster. She knew her biological clock was ticking. She could hear it in her sleep. It started ticking the day she found out she'd miscarried last year.

"I don't like mixing business with pleasure. That didn't go well for me the last time."

"Don't bring him up," Cree said. "Besides you've already mixed it, so you might as well shake it up and see what you get."

"He lives in New Jersey," Brooke added as a disqualifier.

"Even better. If he's a buster you don't have to see him every day."

"I've never had a long distance relationship."

"You haven't had any kind of relationship other than…what was his name?" She almost sounded convincing about not remembering it. As if anyone in the family could forget her ex-husband.

"Anyway, it's been over a year since you separated and more than six months since the divorce, so it would seem to me, long distance is better than nothing."

Brooke heard background noise that sounded like a voice on an intercom system. "Where are you?"

"Picking up someone at the airport. I've got to go. Call me when you get home tonight okay. We can finish this conversation."

"No, it's finished. I'll call you, but really, I think I'll put him out of my mind."

"Good luck with that. Love you." Cree ended the call.

Brooke stood and walked to the large window across the room and looked out at the city. She could see everything from this window. Downtown MoBay and her apartment community. The ocean. The view of the beach was amazing. She could even see the restaurant she and Marcus had dined at.

She should have known having dinner with him was dangerous. That one night seemed to have changed her life. It had been nearly three months and she was still thinking about it every day.

"I can't look at this anymore." Marcus stood. "I'm starving and I need some exercise."

Brooke put down her pen. She had to admit she was on the verge of hitting the vending machine herself, but she'd done that at lunch. She yearned for a real meal.

"Let's go eat and take a walk. Once our heads are clear, we can come back and finish the summary."

Her eyes slid to the wall clock. "It's nearly seven now. Maybe if we –,"

Marcus placed his palms on the table and leaned close to her. "I can't, Brooke. I'm starving. When I get like this I'm not worth squat and I'm mean too." As if on cue, his stomach roared like he had a lion in his belly.

She raised an eyebrow. "Okay, I get the point." A tiny bit uncomfortable with his proximity, she stood and picked up her purse. "So, we meet back here at what 8:15?"

Marcus frowned. "Meet back? Why can't we go together?"

Brooke swallowed. That was a stupid thing to say, but she wasn't going to assume he wanted to eat with her. There were women in half the cubicles in the building who wanted to have dinner with Marcus Thompson. She wouldn't be surprised if he was receiving interoffice envelopes with underwear and telephone numbers inside.

"Let's go to the Water Grille. I ate there a few weeks ago. The food is great and it's walking distance. We don't even have to bother with my car."

She'd passed the Water Grille on her way to work every day and had yet to try it, so she agreed.

The walk to the restaurant was short. They made small talk about the beaches, the food and the music. Marcus had been to the island several times before on vacation, staying mostly in Negril, where the beaches were incredible and the atmosphere laid back.

"We're both off on Sunday. We should go. We could drive down for the day, sample all the jerk pork we can stand and spend a few hours on the beach. You can't come to Jamaica and not see the beaches of Negril."

Brooke had been non-committal. She wasn't sure if spending the day at the beach with Marcus was a good idea. At some point during the day he was going to take off his clothes to get in the water and she'd have to suffer through looking at his chest. And suffer it would be, because it didn't take a huge imagination to conjure up the memories of his buff chest under his fitted, athletic cut dress shirts. She took care of her body, walking and fitting the gym in at least three times a week, but this brother had to spend mad time in the gym. She wasn't *trying to see him that way and then have to come back to office and sit in business meetings with him.*

"Brooke." She heard him say her name.

"I'm sorry, what were you saying?"

"Do you sleep walk too?"

"No, I have some things on my mind."

Marcus smiled. "This meal should distract you."

They arrived at the restaurant.

They ate and talked and ate and talked some more. Once dinner was over they returned to the office and found they'd locked themselves out of the conference room where they'd been working, so they couldn't finish anyway. Marcus retrieved his rental car and offered her a ride home. Once they arrived, he saw the beach behind the community, parked and begged to spend some time near the water. It was early. She could hardly say no and it felt awkward not joining him. Even though it wasn't technically her home, it was her place, so she followed him.

Somehow five minutes on the beach turned into hours. He'd walked her to her door and talked himself inside under the guise of needing to use the restroom. He hadn't been in the apartment five minutes and she'd allowed him to kiss her. And a kiss it was. It was magical. It felt like his lips were made to go with hers, but that wasn't what did Brooke in. It was what he said when he spoke against her lips, "I've wanted to do this since the first time I laid eyes on you." The husky fervor of his tone made her melt even more. What was she doing? She was on one of the most romantic islands in the world with the most handsome man she'd ever known in person and he was kissing her. She pulled back.

"I'm sorry," Marcus said.

The apology caught her off guard. What exactly was he sorry for? She wanted to ask, but didn't dare.

"I feel like I might need to slow down."

She raised a hand and stepped out of the small box he'd had her trapped in. "It's okay. I'm a big girl. I can handle a little kiss."

Marcus chuckled. "Little kiss. I know you must be kidding. I felt the earth move."

Avoiding his eyes for fear they'd give confirmation, she reached up to pat her hair back in place.

Marcus took her hand and pulled her back into his embrace. His face was inches from hers. "So did you," he said. "Admit it." Brooke rolled her eyes. Marcus leaned closer. She felt his minty breath on her face. "I'm not going to let you go until you admit you felt the earth move."

Brooke squirmed under his grasp. "I will not."

Marcus raised a hand to her chin and tilted her head back. "You need more convincing."

Brooke squeezed her eyes shut. He convinced her alright. He'd convinced her over and over and over again until she had to kick him out of her apartment. She avoided him at the office, refused to take his calls unless they were work related and then he was gone. Easy escape she thought. But it hadn't been, because she hadn't escaped Marcus Thompson at all. Not when she ran from his arms that night and not when he'd boarded the plane and left Jamaica. She couldn't escape him, because that kiss was seared into her memory like a branded tattoo on her brain. The only good thing about him was his ability to distract her from thoughts of her ex-husband.

Her email notification dinged. She recognized the sender's address. It was a message from Sam. *Speak of the devil and it appears*, she thought. She opened the email and replied without reading the contents. Her message was simple: *Stop calling my mother.* She pushed the send icon.

No sooner than that was gone, she received an email from Marcus. It was information about the company's new mentoring program for women on the promotional track. She'd already received it from her own supervisor. She knew he knew that. He was just trying to get her attention, remind her that he was across the hall. She didn't need to be reminded. His cologne still lingered in the air.

Brooke dropped her head in her hands and whispered, "Four days. I'm leaving on the 27th. I can do this." But she wasn't sure she could. In fact, she was sure she was in trouble, which scared her to no end. Because the last time she fell for a man, he handed her her heart on a platter.

Chapter 4

"You can do this," Marcus said to himself. She was leaving in a few days but that was more than enough time. All he had to do was get her to have one conversation, one walk, one meal with him and he could convince her that he was the man for the job. The job, of course, was being her man and making her happy.

He taunted her about the kiss, but he was the one who couldn't get it out of his head. He had not had one night of peace since leaving the island and leaving her behind.

Determined to escape the perpetual torture, he tapped the keys on his laptop and logged into video chat. Within seconds the face of his best friend, T.K. Wilson appeared on the screen.

"So, you back in Jamaica mon'," T.K. said not even trying to take the teasing tone out of his voice.

"You got my message."

"First thing this morning. A what goin' on mon?"

Marcus raised his hand to wash his face. "T.K., your Patwa is horrible. Speak Jersey, okay."

T.K. laughed. "I'm saying, man, I thought you were going to hang out with Charlene and my clan on

Christmas. The kids are all excited. Uncle Marcus is coming. Uncle Marcus gonna get me something. Uncle Marcus this. Uncle Marcus that. I feel like telling them, 'Look, Uncle Marcus ain't about nothing but that life down in Jamaica, because Uncle Marcus is sprung.'"

Marcus shook his head. "You gotta rub it in don't you?"

"I must," T.K. replied.

"I'm going to miss them just as much as they're going to miss me." Marcus smiled thinking about his three godchildren. T.K. had only been married seven years. A set of twins and an 'ooops baby' right behind them and he and his wife Charlene had filled their desired children quota within the first three years of their marriage. "They're still getting hooked up with their gifts. My secretary is going to deliver them after work. I wanted to make sure Charlene would be home."

T.K. smiled. "I'll make sure she is. Dude, that's good looking out. I thought I was going to have to go to the store and spend a month's salary trying to make up for you being missing in action. You know I'm not used to buying much. I tell them to wait for the real Santa to come through."

Marcus smiled. "Give them a hug from me."

"Will do," T.K. said and then he eased into the good part. "Have you seen her?"

"A few hours ago."

"And?"

"She's giving me a hard time, but I'll work it out."

T.K. shook his head. "You love a challenge. You've got women right here at home throwing themselves at you and you get on a plane and travel seven hours to beg."

"I don't remember your lady being that easy to catch."

"Yeah, but I was younger. I was still running. You dude, you're approaching middle age. You gotta do a little more to run down a woman."

"So, you got jokes."

"Lots about you taking vacation time to work so you can hook up with a woman."

Marcus's voice took on a serious tone. "Not any woman, T.K."

T.K. paused after that comment. "Well, it's time, I mean except for that one chick you hooked up with last year, you've been alone for almost five years. I think you've more than respected Lisa's memory."

The image of his deceased wife entered Marcus's mind. Lisa Thompson died from breast cancer at the age of thirty-two. They did everything they could to save her, surgery, chemo, radiation, and hormone therapy, even had a stem cell transplant. In the end, nothing had kept the monster in remission. He'd wanted her to try some more experimental treatments, but Lisa decided she wanted to spend her final days at home with her family…with him. He remembered her last words. "Please don't grieve long, honey. I've tamed you. Now you need a woman in your life." He'd laughed through his pain and she had taken her last breath. It had always given him comfort knowing the last sound she'd heard was his laughter. She'd told him his laugh was like sunshine to her soul. He swallowed a knot of pain.

"She reminds me of Lisa." Marcus paused and then added. "Not her looks, but her… I don't know. I get that exact same feeling I had the first time I saw Lisa. You remember, I spotted her studying in the library and I told you that was my future wife. I feel the same way about this woman. It's so strong that, man, I didn't have a choice but to get on the plane."

"I hear you. Well, you get off the phone with me and go make that happen for yourself. I'm on Team Marcus. I'll be praying for you, Bro."

"Thanks, I'm going to need the prayers because this woman is seriously throwing me shade."

"Maybe she has some pain in her past too."

"Don't we all?"

"Not like you, brother," T.K. said. "Look, I'm on dinner duty tonight so you know what that means."

"You need to pick up take-out."

"Oh yes," T.K. laughed. "You go get that special lady and we'll talk on Christmas."

"Alright, man. Give everyone my love."

"Will do."

They ended the call. Marcus glimpsed the time on his computer screen. 11:55 a.m. He'd suffered long enough. He could finally get next to her again.

He poked his head in her office and found that

she'd slid out without him knowing. He headed for the elevators and approached just as she was pushing the button.

"Are you going somewhere?" he asked, nodding toward her handbag.

"Yes, I'm going to grab some lunch when we're done."

"Too bad I can't join you."

She rolled her eyes. "Don't start."

"Start what? I'm hungry. You know how loud my stomach gets when I need a meal."

"Then I'll bring you something back," she replied.

The large metal elevator doors swooshed open, they stepped in and Brooke pushed the button for the basement.

"Where are you staying?" she asked.

"The Ibeostar."

"You should ask them to move you to my place when I leave. The housekeeper is an excellent cook."

He nodded. "But you'll be coming back. I'd hate to take your spot."

"I actually may not be coming back," she replied. "The system is out of pilot. It's been out of pilot, so there's no reason for me or anyone from my team to be here."

"Well, I have something to say about that."

Brooke shook her head. "Throwing your weight around."

If she objected, he couldn't tell. He leaned a little closer and said, "Maybe a little."

The elevator buckled.

That was strange. He'd barely felt it move before it stopped. Marcus decided it was Brooke. She had him good and distracted.

She stepped closer to the door, like she was waiting for the ding before it opened, but nothing happened. She pushed the open button, but it didn't light. Then she pushed the buttons for each of the floors and none of them lit. "Marcus, I think there's something wrong with it."

"Let me see." He stepped closer to the panel, closer to her and let his eyes settle on her lips for a moment. Brooke cleared her throat and stepped aside, but not before he inhaled her perfume. Marcus pushed the buttons the same way she had.

"I did that, genius."

"I know, but well, sometimes I have the magic touch." He threw a look over his shoulder. "You know a little about that."

Brooke rolled her eyes.

"We're stuck," he said. "I'm going to push the emergency alarm button.

He did and the small car filled with the piercing alarm sound. He released his finger. "Security will take care of it."

"This car has been buckling for days. I meant to not use it until they fixed it. Now look at us."

"I'm sure it'll be fine. These things don't take long to repair."

"In the U.S. Who knows how long it'll take here. You know they work on Caribbean time."

"This is not the country or the mountains, Brooke. You're being ethnocentric."

"I'm being bothered. I told the office manager that the elevator was doing weird stuff before she took off for the holiday." She paused. "How do we know for sure that security heard the bell?"

"You want me to push it again?" Marcus asked.

"Yes. You never know, they may have been outside or something.

"I think you could hear that noise all the way at the airport, but I'll do whatever makes you happy."

Marcus did so and Brooke frowned. "I feel ridiculous. The entire island heard that."

"No problem. Now they know how desperate you are to get out of here."

"How desperate *we* are?" She put emphasis on we.

"Speak for yourself." Marcus allowed his back to rest against wall and gave her another once over with his eyes.

She moved to the other side of the elevator car, away from him and leaned against the wall. "I guess we wait." She removed her phone from her purse. "I'm going to call and see how long it should take."

Marcus listened to Brooke's side of the conversation. From the back and forth, he figured the maintenance man was at lunch, but he'd been reached and was on his way back to building.

Brooke seemed relieved. He didn't care if they were trapped in here all night, because when it came to Brooke, small spaces worked to his advantage.

"I'm sorry, this is all we have," the hostess at the Water Grille had shown them to a section of the restaurant named Honeymooner's Row. The tables were small and tight and designed so that the couple who occupied the seats were positioned next to each other instead of across from each other. There was no way to sit in the booth without knees and elbows and thighs and hands touching. It was intimate, but he and Brooke were not. They weren't that kind of couple. At least they hadn't been when they sat down. After an hour of talking about their histories, families and education, he wasn't so sure that was still true. They had at least crossed over into the friend zone, but then Marcus asked, "Are you in a relationship? Seeing anybody?"

The space shrank some more. Brooke hesitated like she didn't want to answer the question. He thought for a second she might not. She might leave him hanging, wondering if this delightful creature was someone he could get to know better or not. But then she cleared her throat and said, "No, I'm not."

He nodded. Her intense dark eyes held him in a magnetic stare. "What's wrong with the men in Charlotte?"

"I work a lot."

"Okay, so what's wrong with the men in the Charlotte office?"

She didn't respond to that, but he sensed some uneasiness.

"What about you?" she asked.

"Unattached. I ended a brief relationship about a year ago."

"You mean you broke some girl's heart."

"You'd think, but no. She decided she wanted to get back with her ex-boyfriend."

"That's crushing"

He shrugged. "She was only interested in my money. I was trying to figure out how to end it when she Dear Johned me."

"She wrote you a letter?"

"Text message," he said raising a humorous brow.

They both laughed.

"I'm sorry. I don't mean to laugh at you."

"It's cool. People like that get out of the way so you can move on to the person you're supposed to be with."

"You feel that way now, but I'm sure it hurt back then." Brooke said and he could tell she spoke from experience.

"Maybe my ego more than my heart."

"So you've never been in love?" she asked.

"How did you get from me not being in love with her to never being in love at all?"

Brooke raised her glass and took a sip. "I don't know. I'm not sure what I meant by that."

"I know what you meant. You're one of those women who believes a good looking brother just runs up through woman after woman breaking hearts and never giving his to anyone."

Brooke lowered her glass. "Who said you were good

looking?"

Marcus laughed. "Well, my grandmother for one and don't try to tell me you don't find me attractive. You've been sweating since they hemmed us up at this table."

Her forehead creased. "Whatever, it's hot in here and you're like a human furnace."

The waitress delivered their salads.

"You didn't answer my question. Are you one of those women who doesn't trust men?"

"This is taking too long." Brooke's voice interrupted his memory.

"I left my cell at my desk and I didn't wear a watch today. How long has it been?"

She glanced at her phone. "Nearly an hour."

"We should sit down."

Brooke frowned. "Have you noticed I'm wearing white? I'm not sitting on that floor."

Marcus peeled off his jacket.

"What are you doing?" Her tone was nervous.

He laid his jacket on the floor. "You can sit on that. Protect your dress."

"Oh." She raised a hand to her throat. "I thought you were stripping.

"I can do that too." He smiled devilishly.

She lifted a foot and reached for the ankle strap of her shoe and slid it off. "I'm sure you could. But let's pretend you don't have an ego the size of the entire island and you not assume I'd want to see you without your clothes." She slid off the other shoe.

God she had gorgeous legs, nice ankles and pretty feet. Marcus shook his head, held his hand out. "I won't comment on that. Let me help you down."

Brooke looked surprise. Was chivalry really that dead? What kind of men had this woman been with? She allowed him to help her to her knees and then she sank down on top of his jacket. He sat next to her. She gave him the side eye.

"I don't bite, Brooke. Not unless it's your thing."

She ignored him.

He chuckled. "I'm trying to lighten the mood. You seem kind of uptight."

"I'm serious about my job, but uptight? That's a bit much."

"It's the vibe you're giving off." He careened his neck like he was taking a closer look at her. "Is everything okay?"

"Don't laugh at me. I'm going to sound like a baby." She sighed. "I'm seriously all in my feelings about Christmas."

He waited for her to continue.

"I've spent every Christmas Eve since I was born with my family."

He nodded and waited for more.

"I know it shouldn't be such a big deal, but it is. It's a tradition to have Christmas Eve dinner together."

"Sounds nice."

"It is. My mother, grandmother, a few of us women and my brother, he's a chef, cook a huge meal. My entire family attends. Everyone opens one of their Christmas gifts."

Marcus was impressed. "That sounds really, really nice."

"Does it?" she asked. "You aren't teasing me are you?"

"No way. It must be nice to have that."

She seemed to relax a bit more after he said that because she adjusted her seating and ended up a little closer to him. "What does your family do?"

"We get together on Christmas Day. Some years, I go. Some years, I don't. It's nothing as special as your family's gathering," he replied. "Dinner is a catered meal at my grandfather's house. It's a good caterer but the house is not filled with the smell of cooked food and there's no singing or laughter coming from the kitchen." He shrugged. "My grandfather and I don't often see eye to eye. He's disappointed in me, because I haven't joined the family business."

"What kind of business is it?"

"Television. Thompson Christian Television. Have you heard of it?"

"TCT Network? Yeah, I'd have to have lived in a cave not to have heard of it. Wow! That's you?"

He felt a little proud of that, but he was reserved about it. "Those are my peoples."

"Why don't I know that already? We had that date —," she stopped herself and cleared her throat. "A television network? No wonder you had a gold-digger in the camp." She chuckled.

He laughed with her. He was pleased she'd remembered the story. "It's not as profitable as people think. It's a business but some of it is truly ministry. I'm not going to complain though. We do okay."

"You said 'we'. Are you sure your heart isn't really there?"

"Not yet. I love my family, but I'm not ready to work with them day in and day out."

"Not wanting to work for the family business can't just be about not wanting to see your family. Heck, I have people I can't stand to see everyday, but that's the workplace. So why are you really not at TCT?"

He shrugged. "I guess I want to stay my own man. I want success on my own terms. I'm not saying I can't ever work for TCT. But I've always wanted to see what I can accomplish without having certain aspects of it handed to me."

He could tell by the look on her face that he'd made a good impression and then she acknowledged so. "That's admirable."

"I don't know. It may be foolish. How many African-American men would have liked to have a leg up in a family business? My grandfather thinks I'm ungrateful and that I've forsaken the family legacy."

"This is sounding like a night time soap opera." She chuckled. "The Trials of the Rich and Famous."

Marcus wagged a finger at her. "You're laughing at us, but everybody has problems."

"I'm sure." She agreed. "Does your grandfather have more children or other grands?"

"I have two uncles in the business and their children, my first cousins all work for Thompson, except one, Luther. He started a textile company." He realized he'd forgotten someone and snapped his finger, "And then there's Geric, another cousin, he and I started a dot.com back in the mid 90's, right after college. We sold it as soon as we hit big money and before the dot com crash."

"So, it's not just about success with your grandfather? It's about his idea of success."

"TCT is it for him. My promotion will mean nothing. It won't matter that this division generates nearly two billion dollars in revenue. He won't care."

Brooke's eyes widened.

"Now you understand why I was willing to get on a plane and come to Jamaica at Christmas." He shook his head.

Brooke placed a hand on his forearm. "I know it seems like it doesn't matter to your grandfather, but he's proud of you. He reads the paper. He follows the Wall Street Journal. He knows what GCS is worth, so he knows what you've accomplished. He is proud of you, even if he won't say it."

Marcus took her hand. She was probably right, but hearing the words come out of her mouth made them more real. "I'll believe that when I hear it. But seriously, I'm not having a pity party. I really do understand my grandfather. I'm telling you why I don't do Christmas dinner unless I have to." He chuckled, turned her hand over and stared at her palm for a few seconds. He wanted to raise it to his lips and kiss it, but the look in her eyes said he would be pushing his luck.

Brooke cleared her throat and pulled her hand back. "What about your parents or siblings? Will they celebrate without your grandfather?"

"I'm an only child and my parents are deceased."

Brooke winced like it hurt her to hear that. "Both parents? Marcus, how sad." She returned her hand to his forearm.

Touching seemed to be instinctive for her. He liked that. She was becoming more and more desirable by the minute.

"My parents were killed in a car accident when I was eleven."

Brooke shook her head. "Unimaginable. That must have been so hard for you."

"It was rough. I felt like I was on my own for a long time and then..." he paused, thought about how Lisa had been his family, but not wanting to share anymore sad stories he stopped himself from saying so. "People were there for me, but my grandfather had custody. He hired a good nanny. He was running his empire. He didn't have time for a kid."

Brooke looked hopelessly hurt for him.

"Please, don't pity me. She was a great nanny. In fact, I call her my auntie. My family was around all the time. I had a nice childhood. I didn't have my parents for the latter half, but life was good."

"My family is so close. It's hard for me to even picture not having my parents. Even at this age."

Marcus nodded. He'd often wondered what his life would be like if his parents had survived, but he never gave that too much thought. "I think losing my family is the reason I've always wanted one of my own. I've worked hard for a long time. Spent a lot of years grinding, especially the last five." He paused again and the look that crossed her face made him think he should go ahead and tell her about Lisa. Tell her he was widowed, but he had time for that. Now he had to use this time, the time they were trapped, to remind her how it felt to know him as a man and not just a coworker. "Anyway, now that I'm in cruise mode, the right woman keeps eluding me." He paused for a moment and said, "Or maybe she's running."

Their eyes met and held. Brooke looked down at her hand on his forearm and removed it, but not before he caught her looking at his lips. *That's right, Brooke*, he wanted to say, *That date. That kiss. Remember it.* She broke the stare and changed the subject. "Have you done any Christmas shopping?"

"All done online weeks ago. What about you?"

"I ordered some things online and shipped it to my sister. She's wrapped it and is delivering it all at the family dinner. I'll watch them open their gifts on Skype."

"That's cool." Marcus nodded. "What did you get for yourself?"

She smiled. "What makes you think I'm the kind of woman that shops for herself at Christmas?"

"Please, I can spot designer gear a mile down the road. I know you're a shop-a-holic. It's all over you."

Brooke laughed. "Well, I did get myself a few things from the online Coach outlet and I found a fantastic shop over on Gloucester that has seen my credit card way too many times since her Christmas sale has been running."

He nodded. "See, I knew that. You gonna be headed back to the U.S. with 100 lbs. of luggage. I can see you now, paying the heavy charge and holding up customs inspections."

She giggled and shook her head. "I'm smarter than that. I already shipped my packages." The smile stayed on her lips. He thought for a moment that she had the nicest smile he'd ever seen. It was genuine and warm, but because of the way she moved her eyes, it was sexy at the same time. He forced himself to stop staring and cleared his throat. "That confirms you're more of a pro than I thought."

"So, what did you buy for yourself this season?"

"Nothing."

"You're kidding?"

"I've been pulling long hours and crashing, sometimes on my office couch."

"Wow, it's like that?"

"The rumors of the mess my predecessor left are true. I'm trying to put some things in place so we roll out with the right agenda for the new year."

"Oh, so you gonna show out in the new job?"

"Show 'em they made the right decision promoting a brother yet again."

She smiled at that.

"I did get myself one gift," he said. "Well, I almost have it."

"A first run edition of one of Marcus Garvey's books. I found one in that book shop, Jamaica Books, in Kingston, while I was waiting for my connecting flight yesterday. Anyway, the owner's credit card machine was down, so I gave her a couple hundred dollars to ship it to the Montego Bay store for me. It'll be here tomorrow."

"I can't say I know much about Garvey."

"I know everything. I was named after him. This book was published in 1923 when he was in prison in Atlanta. It's one of many pieces I've collected over the years."

"I can tell you're excited."

"I like being named after such a powerful man. I try to live up to my name every day." He let those words hang there for a moment, hoping to see some agreement in those big brown eyes that seemed to be surveying him. "Anyway," he continued. "I'm working tomorrow, so I'll get it the day after Christmas."

"That's Boxing Day. It's a big holiday here. Will they be open?"

Realizing she was correct, he nodded. "Probably not. I guess it'll be the next day. Too bad, I won't be able to show it to you. You leave the morning of the 27ᵗʰ right?"

She nodded. "I'll be glad to go home."

"Open all your Christmas packages to yourself."

She looked away then and mumbled, "Something like that."

"I enjoy having you around, so your leaving is going to be depressing. Almost as depressing as this elevator."

Brooke cleared her throat. "Speaking of the elevator." She pulled her legs in under her and attempted to stand to her feet, but while doing so lost her footing and fell right onto his lap.

Marcus was happy to catch her. He enclosed her torso with his arms and met her stare dead on. *Opportunity.* He was not backing away from it. "You are such a beautiful woman, Brooke, and you feel so right in my arms. I know we hardly know each other, but I feel like I never want to let you go."

Brooke's mouth fell open. She shook her head. "You should let me go."

"I will if you *really* want me to."

She nodded. "I do want you to." She was unconvincing. She hadn't taken her eyes off his lips.

"Are you sure?" He spoke each word slowly,

enunciating as much as he could, hoping she would remember his lips and how they made her feel.

She didn't answer. She inhaled deeply and a look of confusion crossed her face. Marcus knew how to make things more clear. He arched his neck toward her. He kissed her on the right cheek and then her left, pulled back and looked into her eyes, checking them for an okay. He saw what he was looking for and leaned in and put his lips on hers. Brooke closed her eyes. He was glad she wasn't going to fight the attraction between them. She felt so right, smelled so right, spoke so right. He deepened the kiss and the elevator buckled. He pulled her tighter and grunted the word, "No."

Brooke snapped out of the trance she'd been in. She moved out of his arms and then made her way off his lap. She stood, this time using the elevator wall railing for support. The doors opened. She gathered her purse and shoes and hurried out of the car, looking back only for a second before she disappeared down the hall. He was disappointed, but encouraged at the same time. She wanted him as much as he wanted her. There was no stopping him now. She was not leaving this island until he could call her his.

Chapter 5

Brooke hunkered down in the back of the car and let out a long breath.

"Hard day?" Desmond asked.

She nodded. The day had been more emotional than difficult. She realized that Desmond couldn't see her nod. He asked her this question every evening when he picked her up and she granted him a lengthy discussion about things she figured he'd understand about GCS. "It was exhausting and it really shouldn't have been. I'm not quite sure how it went left."

Desmond chuckled. "It's the holidays, Ma'am. They have a way of adding stress to everything." He pulled into traffic which was still a little thick for eight p.m. "I thought it'd be better for you with your coworker arriving."

Brooke stared at her hands and noted the thought of Marcus made them tremble slightly. She could still feel the warmth from his body as he'd held her, touched her face, stroked her arms. He was so physical, she couldn't help wondering...

"Your coworker was no help?" Desmond broke through just in time to still her imagination. She didn't need to go to that place where she was thinking about Marcus that way. She'd been far too lonely for that.

"He works in a different department," she cleared her throat as she spoke the half-truth.

"Oh, he said he worked with you." Desmond's voice held curiosity.

"He does, but in a different capacity."

Desmond nodded and she closed her eyes. When she opened them five minutes later, she noted the city streets were full of tourists. She'd heard people came to the island for the holidays. After talking to Marcus today, she realized everyone didn't have a family like hers. She'd known that before, but the conversation with Marcus reminded her of how special their Christmas Eve dinners really were. It made her miss being with her family even more. She'd been so deep in her thoughts about it that she'd not realized how close she was to home. She leaned forward. "Des, I'm sorry. I meant to tell you I needed to stop for dinner."

"Ma'am, I talked to Lefa this afternoon and she told me she prepared a meal for you."

Lefa was the housekeeper/cook. Brooke had no idea how Desmond knew her, but she'd figured it was none of her business, so she didn't ask. Not wanting to get to her apartment and have to prepare a meal for herself, she needed to be sure he was right. "Lefa wasn't working today. Are you positive it was for me?"

Desmond glanced over his shoulder. "I'm a hundred percent certain. It's a surprise."

Brooke sank back in the seat. No matter how much she wanted to leave this place, she would never ever forget the hospitality of the people. Americans and the media could say whatever negative things they wanted about Jamaica, but she knew that most of the people had hearts made of gold. She would hardly miss the tip she had in mind for Lefa, but it would be more than a month of wages for the woman.

After a few minutes, Desmond pulled through the gate and into the circular driveway that served as the entrance to the apartments. Brooke gathered her bags and waited for him to come around to open the door.

"I'll see you in the morning."

He winked and said, "Enjoy your surprise."

Brooke raised an eyebrow. He seemed to be awfully enthusiastic to say it was probably a chicken and rice dinner, but she held her suspicion and decided he was being flirtatious again. She turned to enter the building. A figure stood from one of the wrought iron benches and spoke her name. Brooke stepped back a few feet and waited for the person to step into the light.

She couldn't believe her eyes. Today had gotten unforgivably worse.

"I need to talk to you."

Brooke shook her head. Dread spawned hesitation. "What in the world are you doing here?"

"You wouldn't return my phone calls, so I flew in a couple of hours ago."

Brooke clutched her bags tighter, drawing strength from the strong, taut leather straps. "You wasted your time and money, because you and I have nothing to talk about."

Samantha Riley, her former best friend, took a step closer and swallowed so hard Brooke could hear it. "You don't have anything to say to me. But, I do have something I need to say to you." Sam paused for a moment, lowered her eyes and then raised her head. "I'm sorry, Brooke. I'm sorry I stole your husband."

Chapter 6

Brooke felt like she'd had the wind knocked out of her. "You brazen little witch. You didn't steal my husband. You had sex with him and I decided to let you keep him."

Sam shrugged. "That's not what you said the last time we talked, so I thought I owed it to you to say what you wanted to hear."

Brooke put a fist on her hip and cocked her head. "And what was that?"

"You said, I'd never even said sorry, so now I'm saying it."

Brooke laughed, but there was no cheer in the sound. "Too late." Without another word, she walked to the lobby door and reached for the knob.

Sam put a hand on Brooke's to stop her. Brooke froze, turned her head to look back over her shoulder. "If you don't get your hand off me I'm going to snatch your hair right out of your head."

Sam's blue eyes widened and even in the moonlight Brooke could see she'd turned a warm shade of red. She snatched her hand back like she was afraid Brooke would make good on the threat. "I'm sorry. I have to talk to you. Please, if our friendship ever meant anything, give me five minutes to explain why I'm here."

Brooke shook her head. She hadn't spoken to Sam since the day she walked out of their workspace with her belongings in an empty copier paper box. That had been early spring. She remembered now. Brooke had asked her for the apology and it wasn't something Sam was willing to give. "Don't pull that if our friendship ever meant anything to me crap. Our friendship is something you threw away. I don't owe you anything."

"I didn't say you did, but I need to talk to you just the same. Five minutes, Brooke," she pleaded. "Please..."

Brooke stopped abruptly. "You can't have five seconds, Sam. Go home." She turned and pushed the door open. Sam came in behind her and grabbed her arm again.

"Wait," she cried. Her voice bounced against the walls of the empty foyer, but Brooke didn't care how loud she pleaded. She removed Sam's hand from her arm and pushed her against a wall. The collision with the wood made a thud, Sam's purse fell and the contents spilled onto the tile with a loud clatter. The man behind the front desk raised an eyebrow.

Drama, Brooke thought. She'd been here for months and now she'd leave with gossip about a girl fight in her smoke. It was obvious that this heifer was determined to have her say, even if it meant she might leave escorted by the Montego Bay police. She considered letting the former handle Sam, but as she watched the woman she used to call friend pick up her things she was reminded that Sam's only crime was being a menace to her.

"There's a library to the left. You have five minutes," Brooke said and then she stomped away and left Sam to finish gathering her personal items.

Brooke pushed the door open and stepped into the room. It was an airy space with a humongous palm tree ceiling fan, caramel rattan woods and tropical patterned cushions. It boasted breathtaking floor to ceiling gulf views. She'd spent many a Sunday afternoon in this room reading and people watching. She had fond memories of the space, but now like her reputation with the gossipy front desk staff, it would be tarnished by Sam's presence.

Sam entered the room right on her heels. Brooke thought she barely had time to pick up her things. She realized Sam was probably scared she'd close the door in her face or slip out a back exit. Brooke would have loved to do that. But she was a woman of her word, even when she was dealing with someone who hadn't kept theirs.

She pushed the panel for the overhead lighting and claimed the wing chair closest to the door, so if necessary she could make an easy escape. Leaving the other wing chair for Sam, Sam sat and began. "I'm broke. I need for us to sell the house and I have a buyer."

Brooke laughed and even to herself she sounded like one of the wicked stepmothers from a children's fairytale. "I know you didn't come all this way to talk about the rental property."

"Please hear me out. You said you would."

"No, I said I would give you five minutes, but you don't need five because I'm not going to sell."

Sam frowned. "Why not? You hate me. Why would you want to keep it?"

Sam was right about that. If she was capable of hate, that was what she felt for her former friend. But hate or not, this was about money. "Because it's mine. It's an asset. You'll be inheriting your money, but some of us have to work for ours."

The first tear of the conversation trailed down Sam's cheek. She wiped it quickly like she'd wished her tear ducts hadn't betrayed her. "I won't inherit anything. My father took me out of his will when I married Andre."

Married, Brooke hadn't known they had actually gotten married. The knowledge added another layer of crust to the betrayal that hardened her heart.

"I'm not working. I can't pay the rent. I can't pay our health insurance. I can't even buy food." Another traitorous tear fell. "My dad won't give me anything."

Cut off from her father's money? Brooke tried to imagine a Sam standing on her own two feet. It was hard to get the picture in her head, because not only had her father carried her, she herself had carried her. It was she who worked with Sam in the fourth grade to help her learn her lines for the *Wizard of Oz*. It was she who worked for hours at a time to help Sam get down the moves for cheerleading tryouts. She wrote Sam's college admission essays and the letter of reconsideration when Sam hadn't gotten into the University of North Carolina the first time. It was she who helped Sam with research papers in college, prepped her for the job interview with GCS and so much more. It was always her work, her sacrifice that got Samantha Riley what she wanted. No wonder she was here looking for her help. She'd been helping Sam make it over some hurdle for over a decade.

"You have a husband. Why is everything on you?" Brooke almost smiled. She knew that was a dig, because she knew well what Andre contributed. Sam seemed to be searching for words. Brooke decided to help her understand there were none. "I'm not going to sell."

That declaration snapped Sam out of her trance. "It's a fair offer. Please look at the paperwork." She extended a legal size envelope to Brooke.

Brooke didn't even consider accepting it. "Is it more than it was appraised for last year?"

Sam's one word response came out heavy and grieved. "No."

"Then it's no deal."

"Brooke, I put the money up for it. You didn't even have your part."

"Correction." Brooke cocked her head. "Your father put the money up for it after I told him about the listing."

"Well, I talked to my father about it. I told him I wanted to do it."

Brooke guffawed. "I have news for you sweetheart, I'd already convinced him it was a good idea before you batted your pretty little lashes."

Sam raised her chin a bit and her nostrils flared for just about a millisecond. Brooke recognized that desire to defy her words, that yearning to challenge Brooke's allegiance with her father. She'd seen it before, but now, the distance between them revealed more. It wasn't defiance. It was resentment. Sam's bottom lip trembled with it.

Interesting, but she wasn't going to let Sam's father-daughter issues cloud her judgment. "I paid him back every dime."

"I'm not saying you didn't."

"So then why are you bringing it up?"

"Because I was generous once. I'm asking you to remember that and grant me a little grace."

"Grace. You can't be serious. You were my best friend for over twenty-five years. You slept with my husband on what I'll assume was multiple occasions and now you're married to him. I have some grace for you. I'm not going to beat your --,"

Sam spoke through grit teeth. "Stop it. This is not the kind of thing you say."

"Maybe you don't know me as well as you think you do. I certainly didn't know you."

"I know you. You're a Christian and you're the real deal. You don't just go to church. You live your beliefs."

She was sure Sam intended to guilt her into being merciful, but her words only served to make Brooke angrier. "Don't do that."

"Do what? Remind you of who you are? Use

anything I can to talk some sense into you. I'm desperate, Brooke. I flew all the way down here on a loan I took out on my car."

"Well that was poor planning." Brooke stood and walked towards the door. "I'm tired. I'm not selling and that's it."

Brooke barely cleared the threshold of the door before Sam's voice rose. "Andre is sick!"

She stopped, but didn't turn.

"He has cancer." There was a beat of silence before Sam qualified her statement. "Hodgkin's lymphoma."

Brooke made a half turn. What kind of lies and trickery… "I don't believe you."

"Call Charlotte General. Ask for oncology. The nurses will confirm it."

Brooke whipped around now and raised an eyebrow. "So you and that lying jerk I married can make a fool out me again? You don't think I know there are other Andre Taylor's in Charlotte."

"He's sick. You know I wouldn't make something like this up."

"You'd do anything for him. You'd do anything for yourself now that your daddy has cut you off."

Sam reached into her handbag and removed a cell phone. She pulled up a picture. "Why do you think I quit my job?"

"I was hoping it was because your Feng Shui consultant told you I'd eventually poison you with my hateful energy."

Sam made a noise… half grunt, half moan and shook her head. "No. It was Andre. He had so many medical appointments and treatments that I couldn't work. Now we don't have any money and he needs a procedure. We're on the verge of losing our health insurance." She pushed the phone at Brooke. "Look at him."

Brooke closed her eyes and shook her head. "I don't want to see that."

"You don't want the truth."

"This is not my problem. He's no longer my responsibility and you're no longer my friend."

"I know you don't care about me, but you were married to him. You don't want him to die."

Brooke pulled back a little and let a mean natured half-chuckle escape. "Andre has *been* dead to me and so are you."

Sam frowned. Brooke could tell those particular words really cut deep. "This is a different kind of dead. This is his life. If you ever cared for him you would sell, so I can have this money."

Brooke flipped the light switch off. "Go home, Sam." She walked out of the room and stopped in front of the desk. "She needs a minute, but she should be leaving shortly," she said to the front desk clerk, hoping they'd get the hint to toss Sam out on the curb if she didn't come out of the room on her own.

She walked through the doors that led to the path

to the villas on unsteady legs. Her mind was reeling. Andre sick. Andre has cancer. Was it true? She'd seen him six months ago in court when their divorce had been declared final. He was fine. As fine as the day she'd met him in the company break-room. She'd been refilling a coffee mug and he'd been banging on the vending machine trying to get a stuck bag of chips to fall. Their eyes met from across the room and she remembered thinking he was a nice piece of eye-candy. He's pursued her, shamelessly, swearing that it had been love at first sight.

Brooke swallowed bile against the memory. Something had always felt a little off about Andre, something in her gut, but she was afraid of growing old alone. Afraid that no one would come after her like that again, so she ignored the voice in her head and the niggle in her belly. She hadn't listened to her instincts.

She shook her head and kept walking. She wasn't going there. She wasn't going to let her mind go down memory lane to the place where Andre had courted her, swept her off her feet and married her all in the same three month period of time. How she'd eloped with him and stood on an island much like this one in a rented dress exchanging vows with the man she'd hope to spend the rest of her life with. That had been less than two years ago. It felt like forever when she lay in her bed every night for months crying over his betrayal, but it hadn't been forever. It was still new.

Andre has cancer.

She couldn't wait to get inside her apartment, turn on some music, climb into the soaking tub and escape her thoughts. She needed to fight the memories. She wanted to fight the tears that were threatening to fall. Brooke put the key in the lock and opened the door. The scent of baked goods filled her nose. Once she turned on the lights, the sound of the word, "Surprise!" came into her hearing and then through eyes that were wet with tears of despair, her parents and siblings came into focus.

Chapter 7

It was Christmas Eve morning and Brooke was not alone. God had granted her the desire of her heart… to be with her family. Her parents, five of her siblings and two of her nieces had packed up and made the trip to Jamaica to be with her. She was blessed and she knew it, but instead of waking up grateful and happy, she was filled with a sick sense of obligation. What should have been one of the happiest Christmas Eve's of her life was overshadowed by Sam's persistent voice in her head. *You don't want him to die.* Brooke squeezed her eyes tight and flipped over on her side. She didn't want anyone to die, but Andre was not her responsibility. She refused to let anyone tell her he was.

She tossed the duvet off her legs, stood and stretched.

"I'm going to the hotel with Mama and Daddy," Cree croaked from under the covers. "You tossed and turned all night like a dang three year old. I was afraid you were going to wet the bed."

Brooke's parents had opted to sleep in comfort at a hotel up the street rather than crowd into the apartment with the rest of them. They were planning to arrive early enough to join them for breakfast. Brooke crossed her arms and looked back at the king sized bed she and her two sisters had occupied last night. "Sorry, I've gotten used to sleeping alone."

Cree poked her head out and eyed her suspiciously. "There's a little more to that than you're telling. You talked in your sleep. You were practically fighting."

Brooke shrugged like she had no idea what her sister was referring too, but she wondered what she'd said. Had she cried out Sam or Andre's name during a fitful nightmare?

She'd exercised her Fifth Amendment rights last night when after the initial surprise response from everyone, she'd had to insist her eyes were wet with tears spurned from excitement or maybe it was allergies. Her inability to pin down the culprit was unconvincing. Her family knew her and the stress she'd felt those minutes before from the near physical fight with Sam did not disappear with her joy over finding them standing in her living room.

Arielle whipped the blanket off her head and groaned. "Why are you two up? What time is it?" She stood and with steps fueled with morning grumpiness stomped to the balcony doors and pulled on the chain for the blinds. Sunlight filled the room. She jumped up and down. "Oh em gee! Look at that beach!"

Cree raised a hand to block the light. "Don't get all excited you little mermaid. We're shopping today. I've seen some of the stuff Brooke shipped back home."

Brooke cocked her head. "You've seen some of my stuff? As in my boxes are open?"

Cree waved a hand dismissively. "Girl, I had to check to make sure everything was okay. You know you have a time limit on insurance claims for shipping damage."

"Uh huh," Brooke murmured. "Everything better be accounted for."

"I might have borrowed an item or two, but I put it back in the boxes without stains." Cree giggled to herself. "Don't worry. My American dollars are dying to get converted to Jamaican bills. I'm going to get my own island inspired collection."

Brooke chuckled. Cree was sure to spend a small fortune, which would amount to a month's earnings on her meager profit from her greeting card design business. Sharing the bungalow behind their parents' home spared her from paying rent, but she had a car note and other expenses which meant the tab for this shopping spree would likely fall on Brooke when the bills came due.

"I'm getting dressed. Mom and Dad will be here any minute." Brooke hustled to the restroom and began her morning ritual. Minutes after she stepped out the shower there was a knock on the door. Cree entered holding her cell phone. "Is there a reason Sam is calling you?"

Brooke took her phone. Sam didn't have her number. She read a text from the front desk that said, "Samantha Riley requested you call her" and included Sam's cell number."

Brooke shook her head. "She's here. She wants to meet with me."

Cree snapped. "Are you friggin' kidding? What's she doing in Jamaica? Why would she think you'd want to see her?"

"It's a long story. I want to have a good day with you guys, so please, let's table this until later."

Cree crossed her arms. "No ma'am. No way. I'll table this but only until you're no longer dripping wet." She turned and walked.

Brooke sat on the toilet lid and let out a long sigh. She started to bring her cell phone into the bathroom, but no one called her but them and she had no reason to believe Sam would be that resourceful. Taking out car loans…calling the front desk. This was all so un-Sam-like. It was not the Sam she'd grown up with.

Andre. Andre was the kind of man that would make any woman figure out how to get things done. Things like pay the rent alone, buy all the food, have a dollar to yourself. Brooke shook her head. That was who he was and that was not the stuff of a great husband. In hindsight, Brooke was glad to be done with him. She just didn't like the way he'd left.

But now he was sick and he and Sam didn't have any money. She had the power to help them. But she didn't want to and she didn't have to. *Decision made*, she thought. She stood and finished dressing.

Brooke and her family ate a luxurious Christmas Eve breakfast that her brother, Chase, the family chef prepared. Then they decided to spend a little time at the beach. Everyone removed cover-ups and dived into the ocean. Brooke and Cree chose to soak in the sun from lounge chairs. As soon as her mother and

Chase finished what they were doing in the kitchen, the women were hitting every shopping center in Montego Bay like they'd do if they were home in Charlotte.

Cree covered her honey colored skin with suntan lotion and passed the tube to Brooke.

"I'm not colorless like you."

Cree pinned her with a look. "Everyone needs protection from the U.V.'s. That's not a white people thing."

White people made her think of Sam, the only white person she'd ever really been close to. She thought about that flash in her eyes last night, the resentment she'd seen. How many layers of it were on Sam's heart? Was that why...

"Here," Cree's voice broke through her thoughts. "The sun is really high."

Brooke pushed the tube away. "Mom will be ready soon. I'm not interested in having to wash that stuff off."

"Well I know what I'm interested in and I've been patient. Spill about Sam," Cree said firmly.

Brooke raised her sunglasses and looked at her younger sister. "I told you I don't want to talk about them. I've had to talk about them all year. Please, I want to enjoy this day."

"But—," Cree protested.

"Cree, I know you love me. I know you want to help. But honest to God, the best way you can help me right now is to let me have my space with my thoughts."

Cree bit her bottom lip like a chastised child. "Okay, since you put it that way, in the spirit of Christmas, I'll let it go for now." A beat of silence and then, "So, am I going to get to see Mr. Marcus while I'm here?"

Brooke cut her eyes. "Why do you insist on bringing up topics that get under my skin?"

Cree flipped over onto her belly and closed her eyes. "You've been thinking about him anyway. His name was one I recognized in your nightly mumbling. It was followed by a moan." Cree giggled.

Brooke slapped her sister's arm and Cree feigned indignance. "What? It's not my fault you're sprung."

"I am *not* sprung."

"Girl, please, that man's got you cuffed."

Brooke rolled her eyes. Her sister was twenty-nine, but one would think she was still in her teens with all the hip language she used. "Cuffed?"

"Same as your nose is wide open. That's what you old folks call it." Cree reached for her mimosa and took a sip. "You need to stop playing hard to get."

"I'm not."

"You're seriously playin'. You're a woman. He's a man. You're attracted to each other. Why can't you explore this?"

Brooke let out a long breath. "I don't know. Maybe the divorce I finalized six months ago." She shook her head. "You've never been married, Cree.

You don't know what it feels like to have a failed one."

"I don't think that's it." Cree put her drink down and closed her eyes. Her words came out barely above a whisper. "I think you're afraid of him."

Brooke shrugged. "You may have a point. I might be too shell shocked to compete for one of the most eligible bachelors in New Jersey."

"What do you mean one of the most eligible bachelors? For goodness sake, the man's not a New Jersey Net. He works with you."

"It's officially, the Brooklyn Net*s* now." Marcus's handsome face came into her vision. "And he's one of the Thompson's from TCT Network."

Her sister popped straight up. "For real? You mean he's fine and rich? O.M.G. I could choke you." Cree flipped over on her back and picked up her drink. "Only my sister runs from a handsome bizionaire."

"I don't think Christian television creates bizionaires or a least he says it doesn't. Anyway, forget his money. My career is important. I've worked hard. I'm on the verge of getting promoted."

Cree waved a hand. "You and that career mess. A career isn't going to give me nieces and nephews –," Cree stopped mid sentence. "Oh honey, I'm sorry for bringing up children."

Brooke fought to smile and keep her voice even. "It's alright."

"It's not. You look like you're about to cry."

"It's not about that. There's a lot going on." Brooke reached for her drink and took a long sip. "I'm not ready to get in a relationship right now."

"You're letting what one man did to you keep you all guarded. He was a loser and he's with a loser."

A beat of silence passed between them with Brooke considering Cree's words.

"Back to Mr. Thompson," Cree teased. "Why doesn't he work for TCT?"

"He wants to be his own man," Brooke replied and it surprised her how proud it made her feel to say that. It wasn't like she owned any of his success or even any part of him. *Except those lips*, she thought.

"Fine, rich, ambitious and rebellious. He sounds delish."

"And you sound like a man. You have fifty something names for men. Women hate being demeaned that way."

"Girl, men are different. There isn't a man on the planet that would have a problem with me calling him yummy, or delicious or hot. And besides, I called him Mr. Thompson. I'm not being completely sexist."

Brooke laughed, but inside she was wishing she had her sister's carefree spirit and confidence. She once had more of both, but Andre and Sam's betrayal had broken something inside of her.

The conversation ended. Cree sunned and Brooke tried to read a novel. She watched her brother and sister frolic in the water and then looked up at the sky and said a silent prayer to God for such an amazing family and for the resources for them all to be able to get on a plane and come here. She tried hard to be with them in spirit, but Sam's declaration about Andre was foremost in her mind. *Cancer.* How had his handsome body betrayed him that way? And then there was Sam. Marrying him. Standing by him. Behaving like a grown-up. Trying to come up with a plan.

She took a loan out on her car to get here. If her funds were low, she wondered what hotel she was at and begrudgingly hoped her former friend had selected one that was safe. Jamaica, while beautiful, was filled with crime like any other city and a woman alone… Brooke squeezed her eyelids shut. She hated that she even cared about that backstabbing whore. All those years of friendship hadn't mattered to Sam, so Brooke was determined not to let it matter to her either. But she was finding the fight to keep her emotions in check difficult.

Her father exited the villa with the kids. They were carrying sand toys, determined that grandpa and their uncles were going to help them build a Christmas Tree and a life-size snowman from the sand. Brooke leaned back against the chair and watched them for a while. The kids made her think of the baby she'd lost last year. If she hadn't miscarried, she'd be a new mother, a single one, but still, she'd have a baby. The pain of that caused her heart to ache.

She glanced at Cree. Her sister wanted to know more about Marcus and she wanted to talk about him. Although he had her on an emotional rollercoaster as well, at least thoughts of him were a positive distraction from her thoughts about Sam and Andre.

"He's a Christian," Brooke said, reviving the conversation.

Cree's eyes popped open with interest. "Is that something you can tell or something you inferred from his family's business?"

"It's something I can tell," Brooke declared. "He's a nice man. He has a great way with people. He doesn't have a reputation with the women. You know they all want him, but he isn't helping himself to the buffet. I know he reads the Daily Word every day at his desk, because I've seen him."

"Seems like you've been checking him out a lot more than you care to admit."

Brooke waved a dismissive hand. "He's also a gentleman. We were kissing and it got a little hot. He managed to keep his hands to himself."

Cree raised her sunglasses off her eyes. "Yes, he's definitely saved because only Jesus could stop a man from grabbing that big ole' badunk dunk you got."

Brooke hit her arm again. "You're jealous."

"That's right. I'm a hater. I'm prettier than you, but I'd take that booty any day."

Brooke rolled her eyes. "You're prettier than me?"

"Girl, please. Everybody knows I'm the prettiest Jordan sister."

They laughed together.

Breathless, Arielle, the true beauty of the three,

came walking up from the beach. "What's so funny?"

"Brooke's booty."

"Nothing funny about that. I've been in the gym every day trying to make my behind sit up and out like that," she said grabbing a towel.

"See." Cree put her glasses back down on her face. "I told you. You better go get him, girl. If he didn't feel you up, that boy might be Jesus himself."

***

They hit the shops on Gloucester Ave. in Montego Bay. The family had a cruise planned for early summer and the ladies decided to take advantage of the Christmas sales to get their cruise wear. Brooke had already done her fill of shopping over the weeks, so she stepped out of the store to find some bottled water. The homeless woman from the office stepped into her path.

"Oh. Hello again," Brooke said.

"Ya family is here."

Brooke stared. How did this odd woman know so much about her?

"I saw you shopping. You look like your mother."

That was true. Maybe the woman wasn't so cuckoo. She paid attention. "They're here for Christmas."

"God blessed you real good then. Family is

important."

"I know," Brooke said. "I was going to be alone and now I won't."

The woman smiled. "I'm glad they here, but you shouldn't have been alone anyway, Ms. Brooke."

Brooke's mouth fell open. She wasn't sure what to say to that.

"You been blessed. You need to be a blessing too," the woman said.

Brooke squinted. Was this her way of asking for some more money? Although she wasn't an ATM for the homeless she couldn't help but give the woman a few dollars. She reached into her purse and the woman grabbed her hand. "I ain't talking about me. You have a gift for somebody else. No one wants to be alone." She walked away, disappearing into the crowd before Brooke could stop her and probe for more information. *No one wants to be alone.* Who was she talking about?

Her mother and sisters came out of the store. Brooke was still reeling a bit from the discussion with the woman, but decided to push it out of her mind, because the thought that she was indeed cuckoo was all she could gather from that exchange.

"We're getting hungry." Cree rolled her head and cracked her neck like she'd gone five rounds in a boxing ring. "We want to go to the world renowned Pork Pit."

They'd had a huge breakfast and Brooke couldn't imagine putting another thing in her mouth until dinner, but her sisters were always game to eat. "It's not that far down the road. We can walk there."

"Cool," Arielle said. "There's a bookstore I want to pop into. Jamaica Books and Gifts have you seen it?" Arielle pulled out a map of the shopping area. "It's on Coconut Ave."

"That's it right up there." Brooke pointed and the women made their way to the street and located the store.

They walked into the little shop. It was crammed with souvenirs, hats and tee-shirts that could be found on any stand outside the door. It was more gifts than books. However, paperback novels did fill the walls on both sides.

"You and a book," Cree said to Arielle. "Don't take all day."

Arielle smirked. "Reading is fundamental, sissy. You should try it."

"Why should I bother when I can let you tell me everything?" Cree stopped and parked herself against the wall.

Arielle rolled her eyes and went in the direction of novels on the far wall. Their mother joined her.

A man came into the store carrying a courier type bag. He tipped his hat at Brooke and Cree and went to the counter.

"Girl, do they all look like that?" Cree asked.

"You did not come here to get your groove back, Stella."

"Right." Cree lowered her sunglasses and checked

out the backside of the young man. "I ain't never lost my groove. I might try to get my groove on though." She shimmied her shoulders and gyrated her hips.

Brooke shook her head. "You're too much." She wandered up to the front of the store to look at the memorabilia behind the glass case.

"This is for a customer that came into the Kingston store. He already pay a deposit, so hold it for him," the man stated.

"When is he coming to get it?" the woman asked accepting the package.

"Before the week is out," the man replied. "I have to go. It's pricey. Make sure to keep it safe, you know."

She nodded. After he walked out, she carelessly tossed the package behind the desk.

Brooke stepped up, realizing the package might be Marcus's book. "Excuse me." She waited for the woman to look up from the magazine she was reading. "Is that package for Marcus Thompson?"

The women eyed her suspiciously and reached for the note attached. "Why you want to know?"

Brooke hesitated. Why did she want to know? She reasoned because it was really important to Marcus and the woman seemed to be handling it rather haphazardly.

"He asked me to pick it up for him," she said reaching into her purse for her wallet.

The women looked suspicious. "What you mean?"

"He gave me the slip, but I left it at the hotel."

The women didn't budge. "I can call him and he'll tell you." Brooke retrieved her cell phone and attempted to call Marcus. She figured she could save him the trip, make sure he got his beloved book and he could reimburse her, but the call went to his voicemail. "He's not answering."

The woman continued to eye her suspiciously, but then asked. "You know what it is?"

Brooke nodded. "A book by Marcus Garvey."

The woman pursed her lips like that was convincing and reached for the package. She told Brooke the ridiculous balance and she handed over her credit card.

"What are you getting?" Arielle asked.

"A gift for a coworker." She shook her head. "Not a gift. I'm picking up something he ordered."

Cree had joined them. She moved the note back on the package that said, *Hold for Marcus Thompson*. "You're getting this for him?"

"He told me about it yesterday. He collects Marcus Garvey memorabilia. He was named after him."

Cree's smile widened. "That's a lot of money for a book."

"He'll pay me back." Brooke signed the receipt.

"Looks like any other old dusty book," Cree said, inspecting the clear plastic case in which it was held. "I guess rich men collect expensive toys."

Arielle's eyes widened. "A rich man working for someone else. Where they do that at?"

"I'm not sure if he's rich, but his family has some money and he's made some of his own from a computer company he used to own. Your sister wants to spend it. Maybe I should introduce her to him."

Cree frowned. "Puleeze! That man already has your heart and he's already had his tongue in your mouth, so ewww…I'm not going to be able to do that."

Arielle's eyes widened again. "Tongue in the mouth? Why am I not privy to the details?"

"There's nothing to be privy to. It was a business dinner. We're not dating. We work together. That's all."

Arielle laughed. "You worked too hard at that answer."

Her mother picked up the case and examined it. "Looks like a priceless item. He'll appreciate you getting it for him. Maybe you can invite him to dinner this evening."

Brooke shied her eyes away from her mother. "No, our relationship isn't like that."

"Not like what? It's a holiday dinner. If he's away from home. He's not likely to have plans."

"I think he's working."

"The entire time?" Cree asked. "He gets a break for dinner right?"

Brooke considered that. Marcus at her family

dinner and decided against it. "You all are reading more into this than there is. I'm just getting the book so it doesn't accidently get damaged or sold. It's a favor. He'll pay me back."

"I think you should extend a dinner invitation to him. Us being here is a blessing to you. You be a blessing to someone else," Her mother said.

Brooke waited for the clerk to bag the item and accepted it and the receipt.

You have a gift for somebody else. No one wants to be alone. The strange homeless woman's words came back to her. *Coincidence*, she wondered, but try as she might to shrug off the words. She couldn't. She didn't believe in coincidences.

***

They arrived at the famous Pork Pit and feasted on jerk chicken.

"We have to take some of this back for the guys," Arielle said, wiping her hands on a napkin that had no more room for excess sauce.

"You're father will kill himself on this spice," her mother replied, taking a long drink of bottled water.

"Well my brothers can hang with it," Brooke said. "I'm calling to see if they want pork or chicken." She pulled out her phone to place the call. It was powered off. Then she remembered she hadn't put it on the charger last night. "My battery is dead." She returned it to her bag.

"No need to call. I know my sons. They'll want the pork, but get some chicken too," her mother said.

A group of men, five deep, climbed out of a car and made their way to the stand. They were tall and good looking and in excellent physical shape. Brooke's first thought was they were athletes. They had that team look.

Cree raised her sunglasses and stood. "I'll take care of that order."

"Woot! They're fine. I'm joining her," Arielle added, scurrying behind her sister.

Brooke shook her head. "Arielle is taking lessons from Cree. Watch out world."

Her mother smiled. "You could stand to be a bit more like your sisters," she said. "It'd be nice to see you find your special someone."

"Mom, I haven't even been divorced for a year."

"But you want love in your life otherwise you wouldn't have married Andre in the first place."

Brooke had no rebuttal there. "It's not easy to find someone. Men aren't like they were when you met daddy."

Her mother laughed. "Honey, there have been low down men since Cain slew Abel?"

"It seems worse now."

"You know more, because you young folks are watching it play out on Facebook and Twitter and reality T.V."

Brooke smiled. "Yeah, there are like a thousand

cable channels."

"And Internet radio," her mother added. "My point is, baby, you can't live your life in fear. You have to trust your instincts."

Brooke gave her mother a sideways glance. "I did that. It didn't work."

Her mother let out a long sigh. "I don't believe you thought Andre was the right man. I think you let his charms sweep you away."

Brooke frowned. "What makes you say that?"

"You eloped. You didn't want to hear what your father or I had to say about him."

Brooke shook her head. "Is that what you really think?"

"I know my daughter."

Brooke remembered the guilt she felt after they'd eloped, but more importantly that familiar feeling in her belly before they'd eloped. Her mother was right. "Andre was easy to fall for." His charming smile flashed into her memory like photos on camera. "Instincts are subjective, Mama. It's hard to trust them."

"You do it in business everyday."

"I'm in I.T. It's systems and code and programming. Math and science. There's no instinct."

"Everyone makes judgments, even the cashier in McDonald's, so don't tell me you don't go with your gut from time to time and you have to believe you can trust your prayers. God wants the best for you too."

Brooke nodded. "I tend to forget that."

Her mother patted her hand. "Tell me about this young man your sisters were teasing you about."

Brooke avoided her mother's eyes as she gathered the courage to talk about Marcus. "He's a coworker. We had one evening out. We were working late and …it wasn't even a date."

"It sounds like it was something. Did I hear tongue in the mouth?"

"Ma.."

"Hush now. How do you think all of you got here? Me and your father know a little something about tongue in the mouth."

Brooke covered her ears. "That imagine is going to be burned on my brain forever. Please stop."

They laughed together.

"Anyway, he's a nice guy, but he lives in New Jersey. He's a manager and…"

"Listen to yourself, Brooke. You're making more excuses than somebody going to jail."

"I don't know how most of my conversations today have been about Marcus. First Cree and now you." Brooke dropped her head back and remembered the time they'd spent in the elevator. That had to be a two thousand dollar jacket he put on the floor for her. A suit that she'd noticed hung incomparably well. She couldn't deny it felt good to be in his arms. He'd made her feel special and safe even if it was only for a few minutes in a broken elevator.

Marcus was tempting, but then there was Sam. Her visit was like a bad omen; a warning that she couldn't trust her instincts and she couldn't trust men.

Chapter 8

A missed call from Brooke. "Yes," Marcus pumped his fist and redialed her number. It immediately went to voicemail. "Oh, heck no." He was not abiding by voicemail. If she called him, she wanted something. He was hoping it was him. He put the phone down on his desk and willed it to ring again. When it didn't, he forced himself to wait an entire ten minutes before he attempted to reach her again, then he pushed the redial button for the second time. Voicemail again. Maybe she was on the phone. He'd give her a chance to finish her call. This time he left a message, telling her he'd keep his phone on him and to please call back.

He waited and waited and no call from Brooke. He sent her a text. No response. How in the world had he been unlucky enough to miss her call because he'd left his phone on the desk to go to the restroom? He missed when love called because he had to use the can. That sounded like an Adam Sandler movie. What was more messed up was he liked how it sounded, love. He was completely gone.

There wasn't a doubt in his mind that Brooke had the potential to become the future Mrs. Marcus Thompson. She was smart, pretty as she could be with that creamy chestnut colored skin and those dark brown doe eyes. She wore her long straight hair parted down the center. It fell across her shoulders. It was a simple style, but it suited her. If she wore anything other than a light application of eye makeup and lip gloss he couldn't tell and he loved that. The more natural the makeup the better in his opinion, but what she didn't spend on cosmetics she definitely made up for in clothes and shoes. She was a sharp dresser and although he wasn't one to study a woman's wardrobe, he knew he'd rarely seen the same outfit twice. But Marcus had to admit, what he liked most about her didn't have anything to do with her looks. It was her demeanor. She could be commanding in a meeting, witty and sarcastic when she was wanted to be…in particular she was that way with him, but she could also be cautious and somewhat nervous about her work projects. He found the two extremes incredibly sexy.

Harold poked his head in the office. "Ready to go?" he asked, referring the midday security and maintenance check.

They went to the server room. Marcus held the clipboard while Harold called out the numbers. "So, any plans for Christmas or are you going to just enjoy having a day off?"

"I've got a special day planned. I've been dating a woman for the last few months and she invited me to meet her family. It'll be the first time I see her kids."

Marcus nearly dropped the clipboard. No geeky Harold had not just told him he'd gotten himself boo'd up in Jamaica. He raised an eyebrow. "Does she work for the company?"

Harold smiled slyly. "In customer service."

Marcus raised a fist and waited for Harold to reciprocate a pound, but he didn't. *Nerd*. He can't pound but he can pull a woman. Ain't that something?

"I'm hoping a job comes through so I can transfer here permanently." Harold added. "I want to marry her."

Marcus nodded and said, 'I'll keep an eye out for you."

They completed the tour and Marcus returned to his office to stare at the walls. He'd checked his phone about twenty times and still no Brooke. He dared not call again because he'd come off like a crazy stalker.

It was selfish, but he hated the fact that Brooke had the day off. At least if she was here he could stop in her office and spar with her a bit. Connecting with her energy was proving to be stimulating in more ways than one. Everything about her got his blood moving and he liked that. He needed that. He'd been like the walking dead for years. He needed to come back to life.

He decided since he was sitting in the office of GCS, he might as well get some work done. The first quarter projections report could never be too early and in the quiet of this space he could get it done, so he started. A couple of hours later, the report was almost finished. He realized the last thing he needed to complete it was on a flash-drive that he'd left in his suitcase at the hotel. He'd never had done that if he'd been more focused. Organization was a gift of his, but he woke this morning thinking about Brooke and his concentration was shot.

He wondered what it was like waking up to her every day. Did she arise flirty and spicy or was she more subdued in the morning? He didn't care. He'd take her either way.

He picked up the phone and called Desmond to request a trip back to his hotel and then he buzzed Harold to let him know he was running out for lunch. He looked at his cell phone once again. No texts. No calls. No voicemail messages.

"Good God man, you are definitely strung out on this one," he said and then he smiled. Not a terrible thing, because what Marcus Thompson wanted, he got. It was just a matter of time.

Chapter 9

Brooke recognized the company van in front of the hotel. As far as she knew Marcus was the only one staying here. She climbed out the car and approached the van.

"Ms. Brooke, you need a ride?"

"No, we have a car thanks," she said. "Are you by chance here for Mr. Thompson?"

"Yes, he went up a minute ago. You just missed him. He's in room 4211. You can probably catch him."

Glad to have that information, but surprised he offered it so readily, Brooke nodded, thanked him and hustled inside. She thought about the homeless woman again. Were all Jamaican's psychic?

After a very short elevator ride, she was on the fourth floor. She followed the sign for 4211 and stood outside. "It's just a dinner invitation," she whispered to herself. "It's Christmas Eve. You're southern. People come to dinner." She took a deep breath. "It's your mother's idea."

It took her an entire sixty seconds to raise her fist to knock and even still she couldn't do it. She held her hand suspended in mid-air. "I shouldn't be here," she whispered. She lowered it and decided she didn't have the nerve. She would wait for him in the lobby.

The door opened. Too late.

Marcus pushed out his chest like he'd won a pie baking contest. "Merry Christmas to me."

Excitement shot up her spine and suddenly inviting him to an innocent dinner no longer felt harmless. She cleared her throat. "Don't get all cocky. I'm just here to invite you to dinner."

"Just here to invite me to dinner. Did you say 'just' when I've been trying to have dinner with you for months?"

Brooke smirked. "It's not that kind of dinner. You're still in the coworker zone."

Marcus crossed his arms and rested his shoulder against the door jam. She was eye to eye with his massive chest and struggling to keep her focus. "What kind of dinner is it?" he asked with interest.

"My family surprised me. They flew in yesterday and we're having our dinner this evening. I thought you might like to join us."

"Your family?" His mouth slipped into an easy, genuine smile. "That's fantastic. Wow. Nice surprise."

His joy was contagious. She couldn't help feeling good about it all over again.

They stood there for a moment smiling at each other. She shrugged. "It is Christmas. I know Harold has a woman and if you haven't made other plans, you might be alone and that's not cool. So I'm inviting you to join us, that is if you can get away."

"I can take the evening off. That's generous of you."

"It was my mother's idea."

He clutched his heart like he was having an attack. "I would keel over from that jab in my chest, but I realized, you're talking about me to your mother. That's progress."

She rolled her eyes. "If you need to see it that way."

They stood there for another moment with Brooke looking everywhere except his eyes.

"Forgive my manners," he said, stepping aside. "Would you like to come in for a minute?"

"Why would I want to do that?" The last place on earth she needed to be with Marcus was a bedroom.

"To get out of the hallway."

She looked to her left and right at the empty corridor. They had as much privacy as they needed. "I have to go. My mother and sisters are waiting." She began a slow back away from him, down the hall. "Dinner is at seven. You're welcome to arrive whenever you can get away." She turned. Heart racing, she practically ran away.

"Hold on," he said catching up to her. "We're both going the same direction." They reached the bank of elevators and he pushed the button.

She walked toward the door for the stairwell. "I'm taking the stairs."

"Why?" Marcus asked.

"I've already been trapped in an elevator with you this week."

"The third time you get next to me will be the charm," he called.

Brooke said nothing, but thought, *I don't doubt it.*

"I would follow you, but I sense you want to be alone." His voice was at her back. She smiled at his humor. He was funny. He was always making her laugh. He was nothing like her exes and even though all of them together didn't quite add up to one good man, she was used to their types, good looking, but controlled and serious. No one had made her heart flutter the way Marcus did, except Andre and he'd killed the flutter as soon as she found out how lazy he was.

Brooke pushed off the last step. Marcus was waiting for her in the lobby. She expected that, but the corners of her lips turned up just the same.

"Are we sharing the van?" He fell into step beside her.

"No, I'm shopping with my mom and sisters. We have a car."

"That's nice." Marcus reached for her hand. She stopped walking. He raised his free hand to sweep the loose curl that hung in front of her face. "I like your hair like that."

Brooke couldn't help but blush. He hadn't actually touched her face, but she could feel the heat from his hand and it made her melt. He smiled like he knew it and said, "I'll see you at seven." He left through the revolving door and climbed into the waiting van.

"Girl, he's fine. Why didn't you say the brother looked like Idris Elba?"

Brooke squinted as she peered at the van. "He doesn't look like Idris Elba."

"If you can't see the resemblance you've had too much of the Jamaican sun in your eyes," Cree said. "Remember that scene from Daddy's Little Girls when Idris was sitting in church begging God? Marcus looked just like him when he was begging you. I know that beggin' look. Did you tell him you got the book?"

Surprised she'd forgotten, she said, "I meant to, but he distracted me. I'll give it to him tonight at dinner."

Cree chuckled. "Oh, so now it's a gift."

Brooke was quick to correct her. "I mean, after dinner."

Cree shrugged. "Well if you don't want him to open it during dinner you need to get him a shirt or something so he has something to unwrap with the rest of us."

Brooke reached into her pocket and removed some Jamaican bills and put them into Cree's hand. "You want him to have something to open. You find it. I'm going to get some truffles." She nodded toward a store in the distance."

Cree smirked. "I'll do your shopping, but only because I like spending other people's money."

Brooke thanked her and went to the shop. She

entered and got chocolate wasted on samples immediately. Truffles and bark and all her favorites were on display for tasting. They were infused with flavors from the island like mango and coconut. Brooke was in heaven. Chocolate was her weakness. She was determined to retire at an early age, open a cute little chocolate shop and roll truffles until the day she died. She smiled at the thought. For now, she'd just eat them. She went to the counter with the items she'd decided to purchase. As she finished checking out, she heard her name. She recognized the voice.

She turned. "Not you again. What are you doing? Following me?"

"This is my hotel," Sam replied. "I've been waiting for you to call all day and then I saw you talking to that guy in the lobby and then Cree. Your family is here?"

"That's none of your business."

"I'm just asking. I thought you were here for work."

"Sam, you really need to leave me alone. I'm not going to have a conversation with you about my life."

Sam dropped her head back and her eyes filled with water. "Andre begged me not to try this. He said you'd be too angry, but I told him, I know her. I know the kind of person she really is." Sam gasped for air and reached into her purse for a tissue. "I want to be with him on Christmas. I don't want him to be alone. It could be his last one."

"Then go home," Brooke insisted.

"I can't go home with nothing. I'm in a bigger

hole than I came here in. Now I have the loan on the car."

A pause then, "Call your father. He may have been angry with you, but I'm sure if you talk to him--"

Sam guffawed. "My father called me a slut and told me he never wanted to see me again." She swiped the tissue under her running nose. "You were always his favorite and I hurt you, so I'm done. He said he'd leave his money to the humane society before he gave it to me." Sam winced, took a few deep breaths and began to really sob.

Like all the other stores in shopping center, the shop was crowded. Brooke looked around at the customers and staff. All eyes were trained on them. "You're making a scene." Brooke walked out of the store. Sam followed. "I don't know how to make it any clearer to you. You made a mistake coming here."

"You're not heartless. You'll change your mind and it'll be too late for this offer."

Brooke stopped walking and turned. "You don't know me like you think you do."

"Yes, I do," Sam sobbed. "I know I shocked you last night—"

Brooke interrupted, "You shocked me last year."

Sam took a deep breath. "You're going to change your mind. You're going to do the right thing. You always do."

"And you're not going to use that to your advantage—,"

"Brooke."

The voice came from behind her. She turned. Marcus was standing there. His eyes swept between them. He looked confused by the red faced, crying woman. "Is everything okay?"

"Everything's fine." Brooke turned her back to Sam. "This is an old friend, who's now no longer friend. It's a long story. What are you doing here? I saw you leave."

"I forgot something in the safe," he said, patting the pocket of his suit jacket. "I had to come back for it."

Brooke put a hand on his forearm. "Let's go."

"No," Sam cried pulling Brooke's hand from Marcus. "I have an early flight. I need you to do this."

Brooke snatched her arm away. "I told you to never touch me again!" She wanted to claw Sam and Marcus must have sensed it, because he made a quick motion to fill the space between them.

"Samantha." Brooke heard her mother before she saw her. Cree and Arielle were right behind her. Both their mouths were open.

"Mrs. Jordan." Sam ran to Brooke's mother and wrapped her arms around the woman.

"Oh, heck no," Cree said. "Why is this trick here?"

Mother Jordan turned and gave Cree a disapproving look.

Cree shrugged. "Did I ask an inappropriate

question?"

"Might have been the word trick," Arielle whispered.

"Okay, why is she here?" Cree repeated.

"It's a store, Cree," Brooke said. "It's open to the public, but I think we should let Sam have it." Brooke hustled away with Marcus behind her. She was headed for the car, but he took arm and wordlessly escorted her past the company van to a walkway that led to a covered patio on the beach. The area was deserted. Marcus pointed toward a chair and she obediently sat. She tried to hide it, but she was on ten and sick with rage.

"What was that about?"

She didn't meet his eyes. "I don't want to talk about it."

"You don't...Brooke, you can't be serious. You're boiling." He took a seat next to her. "Who was that woman?"

"I told you, she's an ex-friend. She was my best friend until she slept with my husband and then our friendship ended."

Marcus didn't look very shocked. If he was, he was good at hiding it. "That's a lot."

"Yeah, more than you wanted to know I'm sure."

"Not more, just more than you should have had to deal with," he paused. "Why is she here? Is she on vacation?"

"No, she came to talk to me."

"Really? How did she know where you were?"

"She used to work for GCS. She still has people she knows at the company. I'm sure they told her about my assignment."

"So, she just showed up?"

Brooke didn't respond.

"Tell me what's going on. Let me help you."

Brooke hesitated and then decided to tell him. He seemed to really care. "She and I own some property together. A house that we rent as two apartment units. She wants to sell it and she can't without my consent."

Marcus looked confused. "I would think you wouldn't want to be tied to her anymore, so why not sell?"

"The property value is down. We won't get much for it." Brooke looked him in the eye for a second and then looked away. He didn't say anything, but she could read his mind. "I'm not rich like you. I don't squander money."

"But there's so much bad blood. She must be pretty desperate if she came all the way to Jamaica to ask you to sell."

"She's been trying to reach me for a few months. She needs the money, so she thought she could take advantage of the Christmas season and get me to give in."

"What else is going on, Brooke?"

Tears threatened to come, but she fought them.

"Why does it matter?"

"Because this story doesn't make sense. And I don't know, you're angry, but you also look...I don't know, kind of guilty."

"What do you mean I look guilty? You don't even know me like that?"

"I know people and I know you don't look yourself."

Brooke's hands turned to fists in her lap. "I'm not guilty. I'm not doing anything wrong. It's my property. She can't buy me out, and I see no reason to take a loss because they have a bad situation."

"Did she at least get a fair price?"

"I don't know. I didn't ask her."

"Then it's not about the money if you didn't ask."

"Why are we still talking about this?" she stood.

"Because it takes a lot of nerve for a woman who slept with her friend's husband to pick up the telephone and call, forget get on a plane and fly all the way to another country. She's pretty desperate. Tell me why?"

Brooke hesitated. "My ex-husband, Andre is sick. He's not working and they're struggling to pay their bills and pay his medical expenses."

"Oh..."

Brooke didn't meet his eyes.

"What kind of sick?"

"She says he has cancer."

"And still your answer is no."

"I don't owe them anything. Maybe they've made a hard bed and they need to lie in it."

"Baby, you don't mean that."

"I don't owe them security. It's my property. I'll sell it when I'm ready, not before. Not because they need it. His health stopped being my problem when he left me, so let her figure something else out."

The look in Marcus's eyes made her feel like a bitter old fool. She resented his position when he hadn't endured the betrayal. "Stop judging me." The plea sounded weak, even to her own ears.

"I'm not judging you."

"Yes, you are." She was trembling when she continued, "I don't owe them. If anyone owes, they owe me. I lost a husband. A baby. My dreams, because they couldn't keep their hands off of each other and now less than a year later, they want my money. Why not just ask me for a kidney or a lung? My God how much do I have to give to them before they're satisfied?" Tears streamed down her face.

Marcus stood and took her in his arms. "I'm sorry about the baby. I don't mean to make you feel bad, but I've lost someone to cancer. I would have done anything to save my wife's life, so I understand why she's here."

Brooke pulled back a little so she could look into his eyes. "You had a wife?"

"Her name was Lisa and she's been gone five years." He put a hand on her chin and used a thumb to wipe a tear from her lip. "I know they've hurt you, but I'd like you to think about how horrible you'll feel if he dies."

That angered her. She pulled away from him. "He's already dead to me."

Marcus shook his head and pulled her back into his arms. He squeezed her tight and she began to cry again. "No, babe, he's not dead to you. He's very much alive. I know what he did was bad, but you have to forgive him, because holding on to this anger is hurting you more than it's hurting them. Look at you."

Brooke grabbed his jacket with her fist and held on for dear life while her body wracked from the sobs. "I lost everything."

"I know, but you were strong. You're still standing even though they did you dirty." He released his grip and pulled her away from him and leaned close to her face. "And you're better off without both of them." He removed a handkerchief from his jacket pocket, unfolded it and began to wipe her face.

She took it from him and blew her nose hard. "Men your age don't use handkerchiefs." A smiled broke through as she said the words.

"They do if they were raised by an old man who insisted." He chuckled. "A smile and tease. That's the Brooke I know." He pulled her back into his arms, kissed her on the top of the head. "Let him go," he said. "Let him go, because I'm ready to take his place. I'm ready to love you."

Brooke allowed herself to fold into his body. He

felt so good and so strong. She needed him. She raised her head from his chest. In the distance, she thought she saw the homeless woman. Her words came back to her memory: *God is going to bless you with love*. She blinked and realized it wasn't her after-all. She pulled back and looked into Marcus's eyes. He smiled, but it didn't squelch the heaviness in her heart.

Chapter 10

The women stopped at coffee shop before going back to the apartment, because Brooke's mother wanted the conversation they had to have to happen outside of her husband's earshot. "Tell me what you're thinking," her mother pleaded.

"I'm thinking I should keep my investment," Brooke replied.

"Will the mortgage be paid off?" Arielle's master's degree in finance was asking the question now.

Brooke nodded. "It was really cheap and even though the market isn't great, we've got some pretty good equity in it."

Arielle nodded. "So, you're not losing money."

"The only thing she'd lose is her last connection to Andre and Sam," Cree said, interrupting.

Brooke cut her eyes to hers. "This is a business decision."

It was her mother's voice this time. "Are you sure about that?"

"I'm certain," Brooke said, defensively. "In three or four years it could be worth twenty or thirty thousand more. Real-estate in that area is coming back fast."

No one said anything, so she continued, "I worked really hard to pay that mortgage in the beginning, and even harder to pay for the repairs and upgrades. I've been counting on the money from the sale of that property to help me start my own business in a few years, so I'm not giving in because Andre is sick and Sam doesn't know what else to do. I don't owe her anything. I don't care about her and I don't care about him!"

Cree took a sip of her coffee. "So why are you yelling?"

Brooke closed her eyes and shook her head. First Marcus, now her family. She couldn't take this. Couldn't they see? Couldn't they understand that she was right? "I want today to be about my family. Not about them, so can we please pretend we didn't see Sam."

"I don't think so," Arielle replied. "If you're not losing money --,"

"It shouldn't be about the money," Cree stated.

Brooke shook her head. "Of course it should. If I could shoot both of them I would, so I could have all of it."

Her mother eyes popped out her head.

Cree laughed. "You've got to give that one to her. Kill the ho' and get it all."

"Cree, I didn't raise you to say such things. To think such things."

"Mama, please! Stop being such a saint. You don't know what she's been through. You've loved one man your entire life. You don't know what it's like to give someone your whole heart, to trust them and then be put out with the trash."

Everyone looked at Cree. Brooke was shocked her sister had spoken about being hurt with so much passion. What didn't she know about her sister's carefree love life?

Cree cleared her throat. "I agree that she should sell it, but only because the two of them are poison. She needs to get them completely out of her life. Her selling should be about her, not them."

Brooke opened and closed her hand around Marcus's soiled handkerchief. She could still hear his voice. *Think about how horrible you'll feel if he dies.* Her mother's word's interrupted her thoughts.

"Andre is someone she once cared for and he's sick. She can make a difference. I taught you girls, my children, to always try to make a difference."

"Andre is an ex-husband," Cree interjected. "She tried to make a difference with him already, so to think she should sell because he's sick or Sam needs money is ridiculous."

"Really," her mother said. "It doesn't matter that he's dying."

Cree smirked. "God don't like ugly."

"So people with cancer are being punished?"

Cree's mouth dropped open. "I didn't mean it that way."

"It's what you said."

She snapped. "I didn't mean it. I just want my sister to be happy again. I want her to have love in her life. I want what they did to her to go away." She stood and stomped off in the direction of the car.

"This is hard for her. She loves you almost as much as I do," her mother said. "But, baby, that man is dying."

"Sam says he's dying," Brooke shrugged. "She can't be trusted."

"I saw pictures of him."

Brooke looked away, her anger made it hard for her to hear.

"She says he needs a bone marrow transplant. It may already be too late."

Brooke raised her eyes and looked her mother squarely in hers. "It's not my problem."

Her mother squeezed her hand. "No more talk about it. You know what you should do. Let's get back. Your brother has been working hard and the rest of the meal should have been delivered. I want to help him set up." She stood. Brooke could feel her disappointment weighing heavily in the air above her and she saw it in her mother's footsteps as she left the table.

"Shoot 'em both and get all the money?" Arielle giggled.

Brooke smiled for the first time since she'd seen Sam in the store. "Girl, it's a good thing I don't own a gun."

They stood and walked to the car.

Chapter 11

Marcus slipped into the car singing. "It's beginning to look a lot like Christmas."

Desmond laughed. "Are we going to your hotel, sir?"

"No," Marcus replied. "We're going to Ms. Jordan's apartment. I'm invited to Christmas Eve dinner."

Desmond laughed. "Good for you, sir."

"I'd like to stop by a bakery. I need a dessert."

"I know the perfect place," Desmond replied, "but trust me, they have a heap of food. They don't need a dessert."

Marcus frowned. "I can't go empty handed."

Desmond shrugged. "I'm telling you. They don't need a dessert. I'm sure Ms. Brooke will be glad to see you."

Marcus leaned forward, not sure that was true after the advice he'd given her today. He leaned back against the seat and told Desmond to skip the bakery. He decided for once to let good manners go. It was six thirty and traffic was still slow and thick. He was already going to be late. Stopping would make it worse. Besides, he wasn't completely empty handed.

He reached into his pocket and removed a small gift-wrapped box he'd tucked there. A present for Brooke. Diamond earrings. He'd had no idea what to get her, but he'd never known a woman who didn't like diamonds, so he was sure the earrings would do.

They arrived at her complex ten minutes after seven. Marcus rang the bell and the door swung open. The Temptations, "Give Love" filled the breezeway. A man who looked about sixty years old wearing a red Santa hat was standing there holding a cup of eggnog. "Nathaniel Jordan, Brooke's father. You must be Marcus." He extended his hand and Marcus shook it. "Come on in."

Marcus was impressed with how quickly and successfully the Jordan family turned the apartment into Christmas town. The six foot tall tree was the largest and most notable addition. Second, were the wreaths on the windows and the lighted garland pinned against the chair rail in the dining room and the Christmas stockings; large ones and small ones were hung in various locations around the room. It was simple, but pretty and festive.

The women, Brooke included, were still working on the tree. He could see from Brooke's profile that she was smiling. It was the largest smile he'd ever seen and he could tell the angry and hurt woman from earlier today was a genie that had been put back in her bottle. Someone said something funny and she tossed her head back from laughter.

"You can go ahead in," her father said. "Help yourself to some punch or eggnog, both are on the buffet there." He pointed to a server on the backside of the kitchen island.

Marcus nodded and thanked him. It had been a long time since he'd had to impress a woman's father.

One of Brooke's sisters tapped her on the arm and Brooke looked over her shoulder at him. He nodded and smiled. Brooke smiled back and it did something to him; took the air right out of his lungs.

Brooke stood from her bended knee position and came to greet him. "Glad you could make it."

She was still smiling. He could see she was one hundred times more relaxed than she'd been earlier, but fine lines of worry still held her eyes and mouth captive. This ordeal with her ex-husband was taking a toll on her and he hated it for her.

"You didn't have to get up. I was about to help myself to some eggnog."

"Let me," she said and he followed her into the kitchen. She dipped a ladle into a punch bowl and filled a cup for him.

"Are you okay?" he asked taking it from her hand.

She rotated her head and let it hang back before answering. "I need a day at the spa. Other than that, I think I'll be fine."

"I know you have a lot on your mind."

She nodded. "Not as much as you think." She paused for a moment. "Come on...meet my family."

They joined the group in the living room. Marcus met the Jordans and decided he couldn't think of a nicer group of people to spend Christmas Eve with.

He'd never seen so much warmth and love shared between a family in his life. He remembered his parents being tender toward each other, and he had mad love for his cousins and aunts and uncles, but the Jordan Clan was a special group.

Dinner was a feast. Brooke's older brother, Chase, prepared half of the meal. Brooke's housekeeper, Lefa, prepared the other half, mostly Jamaican dishes. The meal included a garlic roasted pork shoulder, Escovitch fish, coconut shrimp, Gunga rice and peas, grilled plantains, callaloo, mango salad and an assortment of other side items and Jamaican beverages. Desmond had been right about the deserts. He counted three different kinds of pie and four cakes. It was enough to feed a small army.

Marcus found that he slid into conversation with them easily. The entire family had lots of questions about TCT, but he didn't mind answering them. The more they asked, the more pride he felt about the answers he could deliver. TCT had great programming and that was acknowledged at the table. When he wasn't talking, he watched them interact with each other. They were like something you'd see in a Hallmark movie. He couldn't imagine how cool it was, multiplied by the family who weren't present. And as if he'd read his mind, Brooke's brother, Drake, said, "Okay, everyone is stuffed, so before we open gifts and y'all all get itis, let's go ahead and Skype with everybody back home. They should be waiting for us."

Drake reached for the remote and powered on the television. The family stood and poured on and around the sofa. Marcus hung back, but Brooke's mother grabbed his hand and pulled him into the group before she claimed a seat on the sofa next to her husband. After about sixty seconds, the television screen filled with a large group of people, there had to be at least thirty of them. They mirrored the features, complexions and smiles of the Jordans in front of him.

"Hey now," Brooke's father said. "You all look like you've gained ten pounds since Thanksgiving." The laughter and chatter back and forth began.

"Who's that?" Marcus heard one of the teenage girls ask. She was chastised for pointing, but then everyone's eyes were on him.

Cree volunteered. "This is Brooke's friend, Marcus Thompson. They work together." Her tone hinted more. A few whispers and head nods filled the screen.

"Don't work too hard Brookie," her grandmother said, "All work and no play won't get me great-grandchildren."

Both rooms filled with laughter. Brooke blushed. She looked up at him and rewarded him with a smile. He took her hand and squeezed. Surprised that she allowed him to hold it, he exhaled. Ex-husband drama and all, she felt right and now her family felt right.

"We're going to open gifts. We'll see you all tomorrow evening," Brooke's father announced ending the gathering. A melody of goodbyes and love yous filled the room and Drake pressed the power button to turn off the remote.

Christmas music piped from speakers again.

Brooke's mother and brother went to the kitchen and returned with a tray loaded with slices of pies and cakes. They also had a tray with mugs of coffee and milk.

Everyone took their seats. Brooke didn't move, so he stood behind the sofa with her.

"This is my very favorite part of the evening," her mother announced. "Marcus, it's a tradition for each of us to open one gift on Christmas Eve, but before we open what is new, we take time to reflect on what has been. Each of us shares our biggest challenge for the year, our greatest blessing and what we've forgiven, because in life there will always be challenges. But God is gracious, He provides blessings and periods of happiness. People disappoint us. We disappoint ourselves, so we must be mindful to be forgiving or bitterness will set in our hearts and block the blessings."

Marcus nodded.

"We hope you'll join us in sharing," her mother said with a smile. "And since I'm already talking, I'll go first."

Brooke's nieces were sitting on the floor near the tree. They reached for a large package and handed it to their grandmother. She began her speech. "This year, I am extremely grateful that my son, Gage is home from Afghanistan." She looked at Gage. "I've missed you more than I can say. I want to tell you son, your tour in the military helped me to grow as a Christian, because I've never spent so much time praying in my life. I thought I knew God before, but I'm really connected with Him now. I have you to thank for that." There wasn't a dry eye in the room. Gage acknowledged his mother's words with a simple nod and she continued. "My challenges were watching my daughter, Brooke, fight a personal battle to recover from a broken marriage and a broken heart. She's the bravest woman I know and for that, I'm so very proud." She exhaled.

Marcus could tell Brooke was fighting to be strong. He raised a hand to her shoulder and pulled her toward him with a little tug.

Her mother continued. "And finally, I have forgiven Samantha Riley for betraying my daughter and this family."

Cree cleared her throat loudly. Her mother raised her eyes to her and she threw up her hands. "What?"

"Behave yourself," her mother said. "That's it for me." She opened her present and the testimonies continued. Only Brooke and he were left. Brooke hesitated, so he volunteered. "I'll go next."

"You have two gifts over here." Brooke's niece said and she picked up a box and handed it to him.

"Oh, wait," Brooke said, "There's another one."

"Let him open that one," Cree interrupted. Marcus recognized the devilish look on her face. "The other one can wait until tomorrow."

Marcus accepted the package and placed it on the sofa table in front of himself. "This year, I was blessed to meet your Brooke. While we work together, I admit to having grown quite fond of her," he said, looking at Brooke. "I hope to continue to get to know her better."

"Amen," Cree said. She bucked her body like she had the Holy Ghost. "Hallelujah!"

Marcus was glad to see he had someone in his corner. He winked at Cree and she winked back. "My biggest challenge was getting that promotion I just landed. Lord, I thought those folks were going to work me to death." He laughed and everyone laughed with him and then the tone became somber. "I had to forgive my grandfather for not forgiving me for my refusal to join the family business. I realize he'll never be happy with anything I accomplish outside of TCT Network, so I have to be okay with that." He shrugged and picked up the gift.

"It's from Brooke," Cree said.

It was her father that chastised her this time. "I'm sure he assumed that, Cree."

"I'm just sayin'. I see there's no card." Cree shrugged and reached for a coffee mug.

Marcus removed the gift-wrap. At first he thought his eyes were deceiving him, but then he realized it was the book he had shipped to the store. He turned to Brooke. "How?"

Her smile was cautious. "I was in the store when they delivered it, so I went ahead and picked it up for you."

He shook his head, removed it from its case and slowly flipped through a few of the pages. "That was unbelievably considerate of you."

"It was no big deal. It arrived. I was there…" She cleared her throat. "You owe me seven hundred and eighty dollars though."

Marcus's mind did the quick math. His balance was eight hundred, so that left twenty dollars of Brooke's own money. His soul filled with laughter and it spilled from his belly. "Seven eighty, huh?" He shook his head. "I got you." And then his voice became serious. "I appreciate you doing that for me. It was kind."

Their eyes connected like they were the only people in the room. They stayed on each other probably longer than they should have. Marcus broke the stare; put the book back in the box and on the table. "Thank you all for allowing me to be a part of this. I can't think of a better Christmas gift than being with a family that understands the true meaning of Christmas."

Brooke's mother smiled warmly. "We're glad to have you. It's been a pleasure."

Her father acknowledged the same with a handshake across the table. Then he said, "Brookie, you're up, baby girl."

One of the nieces reached for several boxes. "Aunt Brooke has lots of stuff. Which one you want?"

"What's that small box there?" Cree asked pointing.

The girl retrieved it and Marcus noticed it was his present for Brooke. "Oh, that's uh, something…I think it's better if she opens it…you know alone," he said.

"Why?" Cree asked. "It's too small to be a copier or a computer, so it's not work related."

"Cree Ann Jordan, if you don't stop harassing that man," her mother said.

Cree hunched her shoulders. "It looks like the kind of box I'd want to open on Christmas Eve." She took the small package from the child.

Marcus sucked in a deep breath. He didn't want to seem flashy. They exchanged nice presents, but they were simple things.

"Well, can she open it now or what?" Cree pushed.

He cleared his throat and decided to suck it up. "Sure."

"Good." Cree passed the box to Brooke.

"You know you're messy," Brooke whispered.

"All the time," Cree replied, settling back against Gage's leg.

"And you're going to pay for it." Brooke added.

"Seventy times seven." Cree shrugged while smiling slyly at Marcus. "It'll be alright. He looks like he has good taste."

Marcus winked at her and she nodded and turned toward Brooke.

"Well, this has been an interesting year." Brooke began. "I'm glad it's almost over." She hesitated again. "My biggest challenge was the end of my marriage. I lost a baby. It was only eight weeks, but still it was my baby and I wanted it, even if its father no longer wanted me." She paused. "My greatest blessing has been putting my life back together. I

thank God for being able to move forward and —"
Her voice cracked. Marcus reached into his pocket for
a handkerchief.

"It's a fresh one," he said. She smiled and
accepted it just as tears fell from both eyes. She stood
there for a minute. Marcus squeezed her hand and she
looked at him. She looked into the faces of everyone
in the room. Shook her head and said, "I'm done. I
don't have anything else to say."

Her mother's voice came sound and resolute.
"You haven't shared what you've forgiven."

Everyone's eyes were on hers. She took a deep
breath and reached for her glass and took a sip of
water. "That's because I haven't forgiven anything,
Mother. Not a single thing and I'm not going to lie
and pretend I have." She shrugged and walked out of
the room.

Her father pushed off the arm of the sofa and
began to stand.

"Sir." Marcus touched his shoulder. "Would you
please allow me to try?"

Nathaniel Jordan raised an eyebrow and with his
wife's hand gently pulling him down, he reluctantly
reclaimed his chair. "I need to see my daughter tear-
free in five minutes."

"Even you need ten," Brooke's mother said. "Go
ahead, Marcus. Take your time."

"Thank you," he said and hurried in the direction
Brooke had gone.

Chapter 12

Brooke stood on the balcony. She heard the bedroom door open. She peeked through the glass window and saw Marcus enter. Somehow she had known it would be him that came after her and for some reason it felt right. She thought about his words and thought about Marcus's family Christmas dinners. She was so glad she'd listened to her mother and invited him, because even if she never saw him again, she'd given him something he wanted, a warm and loving Christmas celebration. He deserved that.

"Hey." He slid the doors open.

She grunted. "My father must really like you."

"I'm not sure about that." He stepped to the railing next to her. "All I know for sure is I have somewhere between five and ten minutes to get you in that living room."

Brooke dropped her head back and tried to smiled, but she only managed to lift the corners of her mouth. "Sitting there, listening to my family share their blessings and trials shouldn't have been so hard. This is what we do every year and every year since I was a child I have enjoyed it." She paused for a long moment before continuing. "My brother has made multiple trips to Afghanistan. He's come home after every tour. I have my health, my parents and –." She paused, water filled her eyes and everything became blurry. "I can't do it. I want to. I really do. But if I do that it will change me. I won't be the Brooke Jordan my parents raised. I'll never be the person who can share on Christmas Eve because I'll be different. I'll be like them."

Marcus took her hand. He had taken her hand so many times today and she liked it. It was strong and firm and sure. An energy emanated from it and he passed his strength onto her every time he squeezed. "I want to hate them enough to not give her the money. I want to punish her, because even though Andre was my husband, I knew him for a little over a year. I knew Sam for twenty-five years. She is the one who betrayed me the worst. How could I not know she was capable of that? Who doesn't see that kind of character in twenty-five years? I feel like such a fool, Marcus." She scratched her head. "And you know what I hate the most? She's right. She does know me. She knows that I'm going to do exactly what she wants."

"That's probably why she was your friend for so long. I'm sure you've always been good to her."

Brooke felt confused. "But she wasn't my friend. My friend wouldn't have done what she did."

He nodded. "A friend wouldn't have, but people get caught up. Who knows, maybe she's always been jealous of you."

She thought about the flicker of resentment she'd seen in Sam's eyes last night. She'd thought about that flicker all day. There was something there, but she wasn't going to waste her time trying to figure it out.

That relationship was over. It didn't even matter.

"I wanted her to suffer."

"I've been where she is. Believe me, she's suffering," he said.

Brooke gasped and raised her hand to her mouth. "I'm so sorry," she said, "your wife…please forgive me for being so cruel."

Marcus pulled her to him, wrapped her in his arms. "It's okay. What you're dealing with has nothing to do with what I had to go through. But I'm just telling you, there's nothing you can do to Sam that will be worse than her walking into that hospital room every day. She's in a personal hell."

"I suppose you're right." Brooke took a deep breath and released the pent up frustration she'd been feeling all day. "I feel better now that I've made that decision."

Marcus smiled. "I knew you would." A beat of silence passed between them before he said, "Now I understand why you've been giving me the cold shoulder about dating. You aren't ready."

"No, I'm not," she shrugged, "The messed up thing is I didn't even realize it. You couldn't have told me that I wasn't over this. That my not dating was about my work."

"It's understandable you know. Almost."

She tilted her head, raised an eyebrow and waited to hear more.

"You should be willing to make an exception for a man like me."

Brooke laughed aloud. "Really?"

"Yeah, I'm the truth, girl. You don't let a brother like me get away."

Brooke laughed again and shook her head. "That was good."

Marcus chuckled at his own joke and took her hand. "I thought you'd like that." He paused and became serious. "I wanted to make you laugh, but I meant what I said. I'm not perfect, but I love hard. I'm faithful. When I'm in a relationship, I'm all the way in. I won't hurt you the way Andre did."

She wasn't sure how to process that. She bit her lip and rolled her eyes upward, then closed them for a long moment before she responded. "You just said people get caught up, so you can't be sure of that."

"Yes, I can. I know who I am. I know what I want. I don't play games. I don't get caught up. Even when you're caught up, it's your decision."

She released another cleansing breath. "I need some time. I have some stuff to work out."

He raised his hand to her mouth and kissed the back of her hand. Then he opened her palm and kissed it. She liked the way he did that. She loved the feel of his lips on her skin. "I have time," Marcus said. "I'm willing to be a friend who helps you work it out."

"Aren't you afraid of being a rebound man?"

Marcus laughed heartily and waved a hand. "No way. I'm going to treat you so good that you gonna be scratching your arm all day waitin' for another Marcus hit."

She chuckled. "That's not really an appealing picture."

"I mean it. Worrying about being a rebound man is for a sucker who doesn't know what he's working with."

Brooke pitched an eyebrow. "You are mighty confident."

"It's in my blood. There isn't a weak Thompson man in the family."

"Okay, Superman, so what do I do now?"

"Go back in the living room, pass me a piece of pie, embarrass me by opening my gift and then I'll take you to see Sam, so she can get her flight in the morning."

She took a deep breath. "And then…"

"You owe me that kiss I didn't get in the elevator yesterday."

Brooke laughed. "I can give you that right now."

Marcus pulled her into his arms. "I've got about sixty seconds before your father comes though the door."

Brooke smiled. "Don't worry about my father. My mother has him in check."

"Well, in that case, don't let me stop you from giving a little love." Marcus lowered his head. Their lips connected and all the stress and aggravation she had been feeling melted away. She pulled back and a satisfied smile came across his face.

"That was exactly as I remembered it," he said. "I came all the way back to Jamaica for that."

She smirked at him. "You came to work. You got lucky."

"No, baby, I'm on vacation this week." His face was serious. "I came to be with you."

Brooke peered at him through disbelieving eyes. "Really?"

"For real."

"Well," she cleared her throat, "maybe you only owe me seven hundred and sixty dollars."

Marcus shook his head and laughed again. "You're something."

She nodded and pulled at his tie until she could feel the warmth of his breath and the heat of his lips. "That kiss was something."

"You felt the earth move?" he asked.

"Oh yeah," she said and thought, *this Christmas wasn't so stank after all.*

The End

More from the Jordan Family...

Live A Little, Gage Jordan's story Feb 2015

Love A Little, Cree Jordan's story May 2015

Laugh A Little, Cade Jordan's story Aug 2015

A Jordan Family Wedding, Early 2016

About the Author

Rhonda McKnight is the author of the *Black Expressions* Top 20 bestseller, *A Woman's Revenge* (Mar 2013), *What Kind of Fool* (Feb 2012), *An Inconvenient Friend* (Aug 2010) and *Secrets and Lies* (Dec 2009). Breaking All The Rules (Oct 2013). She was a 2010 nominee for the *African-American Literary Award* in the categories of Best Christian Fiction Novel and Best Anthology. She was the winner of the 2015 *Emma Award* for Favorite Inspirational Romance and 2010 *Emma* for Favorite Debut Author and the 2009 *Shades of Romance Award* for Best Christian Fiction Novel. Originally from a small, coastal town in New Jersey, she's called Atlanta, Georgia home for eighteen years. Visit her at rhondamcknight.net and facebook.com/booksbyrhonda and join her Facebook reading group for discussions about her books at facebook.com/groups/rhondamcknight/

Books by Rhonda McKnight

Breaking All The Rules

Oct 2013

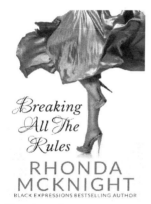

Deniece Malcolm is shocked and heartbroken when she finds out her baby sister, Janette, is marrying Terrance Wright, because she was the one who was supposed to marry him! Everybody knows there's a rule about dating exes. Janette is pregnant and not only is this wedding happening, but Deniece has to arrange the festivities.

Deniece's feelings and pride are hurt, but surprisingly, Terrance's younger, sexier, cousin, Ethan Wright, is there to provide a listening ear and a strong bicep to cry on. Ethan's interested in Deniece, but she has a rule about dating younger men. Despite her resistance, things heat up between them and Deniece begins to wonder if it's time to break a few rules of her own.

Unbreak My Heart

Jul 2014

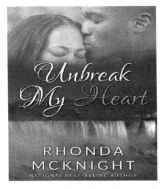 Cameron Scott's reality T.V. show career is spiraling into an abyss. She's desperate enough to do almost anything to keep a roof over her head and provide the financial support that's needed for her daughter and ailing grandmother. When her estranged husband, Jacob Gray, reenters her life offering a lifeline she realizes she still loves him. Cameron has kept a painful secret that continues to be at the root of the unspoken words between them. She's a woman of great faith, but regaining trust requires telling all and healing old wounds that she believes would destroy any chance for happiness they could have.

Jacob Gray believed he'd spend the rest of his life loving his wife, that is until he discovered she was pregnant and there was no way it could be his child. He tried to put Cameron out of his mind and heart, but five years have passed and he still loves her. Jacob risks everything, including his fortune, in hopes of getting a second chance at love. Though he quickly discovers Cameron's not interested in rekindling what they had years ago.

Will Jacob convince her to forgive the mistakes in their past and allow each other to heal their broken hearts?

What Kind of Fool

Feb 2012

The Wife, Her Husband. Their faith. . . . Will it save them before it's too late, or will an enemy from their past destroy their marriage forever?

Angelina Preston tunes out the voice of God when she decides to divorce her husband, Greg. She's forgiven him for his affair, but she won't forget, even though her heart is telling her to. Shortly after she files divorce papers, she finds out her non-profit organization is being investigated by the IRS for money laundering. In the midst of the very public scandal, Angelina becomes ill. Through financial and physical trials, she learns that faith and forgiveness may really be the cure for all that ails her, but can she forgive the people who hurt her most?

Sexy, successful Dr. Gregory Preston didn't appreciate his wife when he had her. His affair with a devious man-stealer has him put out of his home and put off with women who continue to throw themselves at him. Greg wants his wife back, but he'll have to do some fancy operating to get her. When the secrets and lies from his past continue to mess up his future, Greg finds himself looking to the God he abandoned long ago for a miracle only faith can provide.

Samaria Jacobs finally has the one thing she's always wanted: a man with money. The fact that she's in love with him is a bonus, but even so, life is anything but blissful. She's paying for her past sins in ways she never imagined and living in fear that the secret she's keeping will separate them forever.

An *Inconvenient* Friend

Aug 2010

Samaria Jacobs has her sights set on Gregory Preston. A successful surgeon, he has just the bankroll she needs to keep her in the lifestyle that her credit card debt has helped her grow accustomed to. Samaria joins New Mercies Christian Church to get close to Gregory's wife. If she gets to know Angelina Preston, she can become like her in more than just looks, and really work her way into Greg's heart.

Angelina Preston's life is filled with a successful career and busy ministry work, but something's just not right with her marriage. Late nights, early meetings, lipstick- and perfume-stained shirts have her suspicious that Greg is doing a little more operating than she'd like. But does she have the strength to confront the only man she's ever loved and risk losing him to the other woman? Just when Samaria thinks she's got it all figured out, she finds herself drawn to Angelina's kindness. Will she be able to carry out her plan after she finds herself yearning for the one thing she's never had . . . the friendship of a woman?

A Woman's Revenge

Mar 2013

A Piece of Revenge

Where do broken hearts go? If you're Tamera Watson, you go to the pawn shop to buy a gun. Tamera's husband is gone and so is her life savings. With the last of her pennies, she pays a private detective to hunt him down—so she can gun him down. When she finds him, will she be able to pull the trigger, or will the God of her heart stop her before she lets her desire for revenge take her too far?

Secrets and Lies

Dec 2009

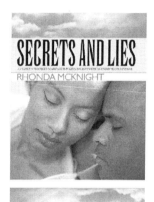

Faith Morgan is struggling with her faith. Years of neglect leave her doubting that God will ever fix her marriage. When a coworker accuses her husband, Jonah, of the unthinkable, Faith begins to wonder if she really knows him at all, and if it's truly in God's will for them to stay married.

Pediatric cardiologist Jonah Morgan is obsessed with one thing: his work. A childhood incident cemented his desire to heal children at any cost, even his family, but now he finds himself at a crossroads in his life. Will he continue to allow the past to haunt him, or find healing and peace in a God he shut out long ago?

www.rhondamcknight.net

www.facebook.com/booksbyrhonda

Made in the USA
Monee, IL
26 January 2022